THE EXPLOSION OF LOVE

"Have you ever been kissed" Pierre teased. But before Zaza could protest, her eyes met his and everything else seemed to fade away . . . her father, the Palace, her life as a Princess . . .

Then, as if it was part of poetry and music, his arms went around her and his lips found hers. This was what she had sought with a man. This was love.

Yet Pierre was troubled. "I have nothing to offer you, my precious, except love," he said at last.

"I want . . . nothing else," Zaza sighed.

Boldly, passionately, he pulled her closer. "Then we have today, my darling," he rejoiced. "It is all I ask of fate and the gods. Today is mine!"

Bantam Books by Barbara Cartland
Ask your bookseller for the books you have missed

The Explosion
of
Love

Barbara Cartland

BANTAM BOOKS · TORONTO · LONDON · NEW YORK

THE EXPLOSION OF LOVE
A Bantam Book / December 1979

ISBN 0-553-13391-8

Published simultaneously in the United States and Canada

Bantam Books are published by Bantam Books, Inc. Its trade-
mark, consisting of the words "Bantam Books" and the por-
trayal of a bantam, is Registered in U.S. Patent and Trademark
Office and in other countries. Marca Registrada. Bantam
Books, Inc., 666 Fifth Avenue, New York, New York 10019.

PRINTED IN THE UNITED STATES OF AMERICA

Author's Note

The years 1892 to 1895 saw a new and dangerous unrest in France. It was called anarchism.

A semi-legendary figure, the fanatical extremist determined on revenge upon the society he hated, was seen with a bomb in one hand and an incendiary tract in the other.

For three years there was a frightening shadow cast over the life of the city, and both the Government and the people became increasingly "nervy."

The Paris press created a psychosis of terror with wild reports that the anarchists were plotting to introduce deadly minerals into the water supply and to blow up the sewers.

After Vaillant's bomb attempt in Parliament, new laws were passed and Churches were constantly being raided, but the assassination of the President at Lyons on June 24, 1894, was the last of its kind for a long period.

After the arrest of all anarchial suspects, no more bombs exploded and the "terror" was over.

Chapter One

1894

Princess Marie-Celeste walked through the long passages of the Palace towards the Music-Room.

She was alone and she thought that on any other day she would have been thrilled to know that she could linger if she wished to, or move quickly if she preferred.

Ordinarily, had she done either of these things, the Countess Glucksburg would have been telling her either to hurry or to go slower and reminding her that the Professor was waiting.

If there was one person who made her life intolerable it was the Countess Glucksburg, with her reverence for protocol, with her eternal reminders that "a Princess does not do this" and "a Princess does not do that."

It often seemed to Princess Marie-Celeste that her whole life was spent listening to the Countess and the only time she could escape from her harsh gutteral voice was when she was in bed.

The Royal Duchy of Melhausen, situated as it was between France and Germany, had a mixed population derived from its two adjoining countries.

Because the late Grand-Duchess, who had been English, favoured the French faction and the majority of Marie-Celeste's and her sister's teachers were French, it had been considered politic for a Lady-in-Waiting to be unmistakably German.

The Countess Glucksburg had every quality of her ancestry.

She was autocratic, arrogant, and rude to her inferiors, and submissive, subservient, and obsequious to her superiors.

To Princess Marie-Celeste she was the unbending, almost inhuman attendant who expected to be obeyed.

The Countess, however, like innumerable other Melhausen citizens, had succumbed to influenza after an unexpectedly cold spell in May.

It was wrong of her, Princess Marie-Celeste told herself, to be so pleased, but it gave her a sense of freedom that she had begun to value more than anything else.

"Without the Countess," she said to her younger sister, Rachel, "I feel as if I could fly into the air towards the sun."

"That is what I would like to do," Rachel replied.

Marie-Celeste was instantly contrite, knowing she had been thoughtless in saying this to her sister, who was forced to rest for long hours every day owing to a weak back.

"I am sorry, dearest," she said.

"Do not be so stupid," Rachel replied. "You know you can say what you like to me, darling Zaza, when there is no-one else about."

When they were alone she always called her elder sister "Zaza," which was a joke invented many years ago when one of the Courtiers had given them as a Christmas present a very ugly golliwog.

On the card had been written:

To their Royal Highnesses, the Princess Marie-Celeste and Princess Rachel, hoping this little token of esteem will bring them laughter, and they will both like it.

Unfortunately the handwriting had been so bad that for some moments the sisters had thought the word was "grow" instead of "both."

Knowing the Courtier whose gift it was, they thought the idea of growing like the golliwog so funny that it had remained a joke which they had never been able to forget.

There was a comedian in Melhausen at the time who sang a song that became very popular in which, dressed as a golliwog, he proclaimed his love for a woman called "Zaza," who did not return it.

Rachel had heard the song from the servants and she began to call Marie-Celeste "Zaza."

"Zaza, you grow more like my golliwog every day," she would say, and the idea made them laugh because it was so ridiculous.

As laughter was a rare event in the Palace, the joke never grew stale, and Marie-Celeste grew used to thinking of herself as Zaza, almost forgetting except on formal occasions that she had been christened Marie-Celeste Adelaide Suzanne.

Rachel was the one person in the Palace, with the exception of the Professor, to whom she could talk, who had the slightest understanding of her desire to know something beyond the over-decorated walls and the constrictions imposed on her.

She had thought that when she grew too old to be in the School-Room she would be able to escape at least by meeting people who talked more intelligently than those who were in attendance upon her father.

Perhaps she might even have the opportunity of travelling as her mother had always promised her she would do.

But the Grand-Duchess had died two years ago and Zaza began to realise that she would never be allowed to go and stay in England or anywhere else.

When her father accepted invitations from the other Monarchs in Europe he obviously had no wish to be accompanied by his daughter, feeling that perhaps he would find the effort of chaperoning her conflicted with the pursuit of his own interests when he was away from Melhausen.

Outside his own country the Grand-Duke was considered an interesting and rather attractive man, although even his most fervent admirers would not have thought him particularly over-burdened with brains.

But at home he was a petty tyrant, bullying his two daughters and treating those who waited on him in the Palace rather as if they were on the barrack square.

Although his blood was more French than German, he admired the efficiency of the Prussians and thought the strict protocol practised in their Courts desirable in his own.

But to Zaza as she grew older it all became more and more intolerable.

Perhaps she would not have been so aware of it or not have realised how restricted her life was if it had not been for Professor Dumont.

It was her mother who had chosen him as a music-teacher ten years ago, and for ten years Zaza had grown more and more fond of him and more and more interested in what he had to say to her.

It would have been difficult to have any intimate conversation with him had it not been for the fact that the Countess Glucksburg was completely tone-deaf.

She was therefore bored with music and, as Zaza's lesson usually took place after luncheon, in a somnolent mood.

Both the Professor and Zaza knew that if they played for the first ten minutes of the lesson, the Countess would then be fast asleep and they could discuss whatever interested them without any fear of being overheard.

The Professor was both interesting and intelligent.

He was not only an extremely able musician, having studied under several of the great masters, but he was also the author of two books on Philosophy and was, as he called himself, a "free thinker."

"I believe in freedom," he said over and over again to Zaza, "and that means not only freedom of the individual but of the mind."

It was the Professor rather than her tutors of Literature who told Zaza what books to read, and it was the Professor who discussed them with her afterwards, opening her mind to new horizons of which she would never have been aware had it not been for him.

Her mother had known and approved.

"The Professor is a very exceptional man in every way," she had said to Zaza. "You can learn a great deal by listening to him, but do not neglect your music. You play very well for an amateur."

The Professor taught Zaza the piano and, because it was his own favourite instrument, the violin, but most of all he taught her how to think.

He seemed to her very old and very wise, and actually at sixty-five the Professor had aged a great deal since she had first known him.

Zaza was aware that it was because he lived alone and half the time forgot his meals when he was carried away either by his music or by some new and original thought which had come to him from the friends with whom he corresponded all over the world.

She knew that he was in touch especially with those who were the originators of new ideas in Paris, which, as the Professor said often enough, was the cultural centre of Europe.

It was from the Professor that Zaza had learnt of trends that would never otherwise have been mentioned in the Palace at Melhausen.

The Professor spoke to her of a new movement that was taking place in Paris towards greater freedom and social mobility.

"A new age and a new revelation is beginning," he said, "and already my friends are speaking of it as 'La Belle Epoque.'"

Zaza was fascinated.

"Tell me, tell me all about it," she begged, and the Professor described to her just how a number of young artists had rebelled against the academic traditions of painting.

This had caught her imagination and she had learnt all she could about the "Impressionists," until he began to speak of the "Symbolists," who were fighting for freedom of the imagination and unfettered self-expression.

She had not been quite certain that she understood exactly what they were demanding.

But it was obvious that the Professor believed that Symbolism was the enemy of false sensibility and that it was trying to evoke by poetry the same feelings as music did for those who had ears to hear.

"There is in Paris," the Professor said, "assembled one of the most brilliant galaxies of poetic talent ever known in Literary history."

Zaza gazed at him wide-eyed and persuaded him to bring her some of the Symbolist poetry which she tried to understand.

She found every lesson fascinating because the Professor always had new ideas.

"Today I have had a letter from my friend in Marseilles," he would begin. "He tells me that . . ."

He would read her his friend's letter and explain it to Zaza, who would listen rapturously until a movement by the Countess would make them quickly start playing again, often to find to Zaza's dismay that the lesson was over and she must leave.

"Thank you very much, *Monsieur*," she would say formally. "I have enjoyed my music-lesson."

"Your Royal Highness is very gracious," he would answer, "and there is no doubt that your playing has greatly improved."

He would then bow his grey head in the prescribed Court manner and Zaza would give him an understanding smile before she was whisked away by the Countess back along the corridors to the School-Room.

Today there was no Countess and she knew she would have been longing to hear more about the Symbolists in Paris had it not been that she had news of her own to tell the Professor.

News, she thought, which made her feel a little sick, and there was a heavy feeling within her breast that she knew was one of apprehension if not fear.

Before she reached the Music-Room she could hear the Professor playing the piano.

He had in his youth had a great musical success in Paris, and in several other Capitals of the world, before he was seized with a wanderlust that would not let him stay long anywhere.

He had travelled in countries where the people had never heard of him, not bothering to give recitals but spending the money he had earned in seeing new places, meeting new people, and expanding his intellectual range.

When he returned after some years, he had found himself almost forgotten as a musician.

It had not troubled him.

He had written a book of his travels, which had not been a success, and later a book on Philosophy, which had attracted a great deal of notice amongst scholars in the Literary fraternity but had not been of any interest to the general public.

It was then that he had suddenly realised he was hard-up and getting too old to start a musical career all over again.

Also, owing to the fact that he had suffered from all sorts of strange foreign fevers, he was not as strong as he had once been and his fingers had grown somewhat stiff.

As soon as the Grand-Duchess heard that he was in Melhausen she had remembered hearing him play when she was a girl. So she had sent for him to come to the Palace and asked him if he would teach her daughters, which he had been delighted to do.

However, he had not expected to find that anyone so beautiful as the Princess Marie-Celeste should also be highly intelligent, and she had in fact after a short acquaintance become the love of his life.

She was not only the child he had never had and who he had thought would want to emulate him, but she was the pupil whom every master believes he can guide and inspire to carry on the message that he wishes to give the world.

"You must fight for freedom of the mind and the soul," he said to Zaza over and over again.

Although she was prepared to agree that it was

something she should do, she was not certain how it was possible for her to fight for anything under the jurisdiction of her father.

She opened the door of the Music Room and the Professor stopped playing to jump up from the music-stool in front of the large Bechstein piano.

"*Bonjour, ma Princesse!*" he began, and looked behind her in surprise. "*Madame la Comtesse* is not with you?"

"No, she is ill," Zaza explained.

"That is good!" he said. "Very good, because now I can tell you my news."

"I also have something to tell you," Zaza said in a small voice

It was obvious that the Professor was not listening.

His eyes were shining and he was looking so excited that she knew it was impossible for him to contain for one moment longer what he wanted to tell her.

"What is it?" she asked.

"I have had a letter from my friends in Paris who want me to join them. Very exciting things are happening and they say it is absolutely imperative that I should give them my advice."

"You are going to Paris?" Zaza questioned.

She felt her heart sink dismally at the idea, but there was no doubt that the Professor was ecstatic.

"Yes, I am going to Paris tomorrow," he said. "I have not told you *ma Princesse*, but I have been planning it for some time. I must find out what is happening! I must be in the swim. I cannot continue to live and die in this back-water."

Zaza was not insulted by the manner in which he spoke since she had heard him say it so often before.

Instead she said:

"I can understand, Professor, how excited you are, but I cannot think how I will do without you."

"Have hope, *ma petite*," the Professor said. "It is sad you cannot come too. You would enjoy the stimulation of intellectual minds when words fly like daggers between two antagonists—the excitement, the drama! However, that is impossible."

The way his eyes were flashing and the manner in which he was gesticulating made him seem far younger than his years and Zaza thought she had never seen him so happy.

But it merely accentuated her own depression.

"So you go tomorrow," she said in a low voice.

"I leave tomorrow, very early," the Professor replied. "I would have taken my niece with me but, alas, she is ill with influenza."

"Everyone in Melhausen has influenza."

"Except you and me."

He smiled at Zaza as he spoke, and she said:

"I too have something to tell you, Professor. I cannot bear you to leave me at this particular moment."

As if he noticed for the first time the expression on her face, he asked:

"What has upset you, *ma Princesse?* What has occurred?"

"Papa has just informed me," Zaza replied, "that he is arranging for my marriage to Prince Aristide of Valoire."

"Marriage!" the Professor exclaimed. "*Ma pauvre petite,* then you will be lost, completely lost! You will go from Palace to Palace. What hope is there for you? And doubtless this Prince is dull, pompous, and stupid, as are all the other Princelings we see round us."

The Professor had a very poor opinion of Monarchy in general and in particular of those who visited the Palace.

There had been no prospective suitors amongst them, and Zaza had found them exceedingly lacking in imagination and usually very puffed up with their own consequence.

She was certain that the Professor was right and Prince Aristide would be no different from the rest. Her life when she married him would be very much the same as it was now, with the exception that instead of having her father ordering her about, she would have a husband to do so.

"It is intolerable," the Professor was saying, "that with your brains and your intelligence you should have to bow to the altar of the Bourgeoisie, who strangle every freedom, even that of the mind."

This theory, Zaza knew, was the contention of his friends, that all social iniquities and injustices came from the ruling by the Bourgeoisie, who filled every position in Parliament, the Courts, the Church, and the Army.

"I am sure you are right," she said, "but what can I do?"

"You must refuse to marry," the Professor replied. "You must strike a blow for freedom. You are only a woman, but a woman as clever as you could unfurl the flag of freedom!"

Zaza sighed.

The Professor was talking in an ecstatic manner which meant he was carried away by his own rhetoric.

She knew her father would not listen to her.

In fact he would be absolutely astounded if she even suggested that she might wish to choose her own husband rather than be married off at his command to a Royal Prince whom he thought suitable.

Because the Grand-Duke was so overbearing Zaza had found it politic not to argue with him but merely to accept whatever he said and, if it was possible, do the opposite.

It was something she had seen her mother doing very effectively all her life.

Because the Grand-Duchess had been a very intelligent woman she had always managed without any difficulty to get her own way in everything that mattered.

This was principally because the Grand-Duke had been in love with his wife and also had a great respect for her.

It often seemed to Zaza as if he never actually saw his children as people.

They were there and he considered them in material ways, expecting them to obey him, but otherwise they were as much a part of the Palace as a chair or a table and he never really thought of them as human beings.

She thought now that she might be brave enough to tell her father what she felt about her future marriage, but she knew it would make no difference and he would not listen to her.

She was quite certain that long before she had spoken even a sentence of disagreement he would be shouting her into silence and there would be no question of their having a reasonable discussion on the matter.

"Marriage!" the Professor exclaimed. "Marriage to some imbecile who wears a crown because his father wore one before him and his grandfather before that! How can you face such a life? The banality of undeveloped minds in the company of women like the Countess Glucksburg!"

It was this last remark more than anything else which made Zaza feel it was impossible.

The Professor was right.

How could she tolerate listening and talking to a Glucksburg for the next fifty years without even the Professor to mitigate the intolerable boredom of it?

Her grey-blue eyes were very large in her small face as she asked:

"What can I do? Please tell me what I can do."

The Professor threw out his hands in a typically French gesture.

"You must escape," he said. "You must escape before it is too late and you find yourself imprisoned in a gilded cage until your mind will wither and die."

Zaza shivered.

She had thought, when her father had told her that her marriage was being planned and the Ambassador to Valoire was already discussing it with the Prince himself, that she was receiving a life sentence.

But now the Professor had made the prospect

seem more vivid, more terrifying, and she knew that she was afraid.

"It is intolerable," he cried, bringing his clenched fist down on the piano with a resounding thump, "that women should still be treated as chattels! His Royal Highness says 'you must do this' and 'you must do that,' and you obey him. Why? Because you are a woman!"

"That is true," Zaza agreed.

"If you were a man it would be different; you could say: 'I want time to think. I want to choose my own wife. I will not be handed over like a parcel over a counter to someone I do not know, or sent to live in a country which I might detest.'"

"You are right, of course, you are right!" Zaza said. "But you know Papa would never listen to me."

The Professor knew this was true. He disliked the Grand-Duke and had criticised often enough the manner in which he ruled Melhausen.

"Your Schools are out-of-date," he had protested a thousand times. "You have only two Universities with bumbling old teachers who have not kept up with the times, and everything new is considered revolutionary or inflammatory!"

Zaza thought despairingly that doubtless she would find exactly the same conditions in Valoire, but what could she do about it? Was it likely anyone would listen to her? No! Of course not!

She might be the reigning Princess but she would still be a woman, and, what was more, when she reached Valoire she would be a foreigner.

"I cannot ... do it!" she said, more to herself than to the Professor, but he heard her.

"You have no choice," he said. "That I understand, unless of course you are brave enough to run away."

"Run away?" Zaza questioned.

"Why not? The world is a large place—a world you have never seen because you have been shut up in this painted prison."

"But ... where would ... I go?" Zaza asked, knowing the answer.

"Paris, of course! Paris!" the Professor replied. "There you will find people, hundreds and thousands of people, who think as we do. People who believe in progress, people who do not moulder away their lives but who live them to the full."

Zaza drew in her breath.

To see Paris had always been one of her dreams. She had read all the books the Professor had given her about the City and she studied every other book which came her way.

But printed words were not the same as being able to use her eyes, to see and feel Paris, to hear its voice and smell the fragrance of it.

"You say I should . . . go to Paris," she said. "Then why do you not take me with . . . you tomorrow?"

She saw the expression of astonishment on the Professor's face and realised that as usual he had been carried away by his own ideas and had not applied them in a practical manner to the subject under discussion.

He was always doing that whenever his idealism excited him and he found it difficult to reconcile the enthusiasm of his mind with the needs of his body.

For a moment there was silence, then the Professor said:

"Do you mean that you would come with me?"

"Why not?" Zaza asked. "If your niece cannot accompany you, why should I not take her place?"

The Professor's eyes were on her face and she knew that he was considering how it could be done.

After a moment he said:

"I have my niece's passport, and why should you not use it? But perhaps we would be stopped at the border."

"I see no reason why anyone should suspect that your niece is in fact an escaped Princess," Zaza remarked.

The Professor was so overwhelmed by the idea that he sat down on the music-stool while she was still standing.

"It is possible—I suppose it is possible," he murmured, "and I could show you Paris, the Paris we

have always discussed, the real Paris! Not the painted
picture of it which is shown to tourists."

"That is the Paris I would like to see," Zaza
said.

The Professor suddenly flung out his arms as if
he embraced the world.

"Then come with me!" he cried. "I will show
you how to live, which is something you have never
been able to do until now, and if I am thrown into
prison it will be worth it."

"Thrown into prison?" Zaza questioned. "Could
that happen if we were caught?"

"Undoubtedly!" the Professor replied. "Your father would accuse me of abducting you! That is a
punishable offence in every country, and Melhausen
is no exception."

"Then we must not be caught," Zaza said.

She spoke lightly, then added in a more serious
tone:

"I think one thing that could save us both from
public exposure is that Papa would not want a scandal."

"That is true," the Professor agreed. "His Royal
Highness is very sensitive to public opinion."

"He would also," Zaza reasoned, "not wish Prince
Aristide to know I had run away because I objected
to marrying him. If nothing else, it would certainly
give rise to an uncomfortable situation between our
two countries."

"You are being very intelligent," the Professor
said approvingly.

"What I think is," Zaza went on, "I must get it
into Papa's mind that I am just taking a holiday. I
will leave a letter telling him so, and because he
always believes what he wants to believe he will not
read anything deeper into my action, although he
will be very angry that I have left without asking his
permission."

"Good thinking! Very good thinking!" the Professor approved. "The question is—how will you get
away?"

"I was thinking about that," Zaza said, "and it will certainly not be easy."

* * *

As the train left the station at seven o'clock the following morning, Zaza leant back in her second-class compartment and thought that "getting away" had been far easier than she had anticipated.

When she had left the Professor in the Music-Room the previous day, she had run swiftly, and in a manner which would certainly have evoked the condemnation of the Countess Glucksburg, up to her sister's room.

Rachel was leaning back against her pillows, waiting eagerly for her sister's return from her music-lesson.

She hated being confined to bed, but the Doctors could recommend no other cure for the weakness of her back and the lassitude from which she habitually suffered.

The hours when she had nothing to do and no-one to talk to passed slowly and drearily.

Now as Zaza came into the room as if blown on the wind, Rachel looked up eagerly.

"I am glad you are back, Zaza!" she exclaimed.

Zaza shut the door carefully.

"Rachel, I have something to tell you, something very, very exciting!"

"What is it?"

"I am running away!"

"Running away?" Rachel exclaimed.

"From Prince Aristide! From the Palace! From this boring life where nothing ever happens! I am going to Paris!"

Rachel gave a little cry of excitement.

"Paris?"

"Yes, with the Professor. He is leaving tomorrow morning, so you will have to help me. There is so much to do and I do not know where to begin."

"What will Papa say?"

"He will not know until after I have gone. I am

going to write him a letter saying I am taking a holiday to think over my future marriage and that he will, I feel, understand that it is a very big step to take without careful thought."

"Papa will never understand that anyone wants to think when he has already decided what they shall do."

"I know that, but he would be much more upset if I told him the truth, that I had gone to Paris to meet people who talked intelligently and who did not keep saying: 'Yes, Your Royal Highness' or 'No, Your Royal Highness!' over and over again!"

"I am sure you are right to go," Rachel said, "but you must not be caught before you can get away."

"That is what I am frightened of," Zaza said, "and, Rachel, we have to think of so many things. First of all, I must have some money."

"Money!" Rachel exclaimed.

"Yes, money. I cannot expect the Professor to pay for everything for me. Besides, he is always hard-up."

"But we have no money!"

This was true. If they went shopping a Lady-in-Waiting paid for them. Otherwise the bills were sent to the Palace and the Master of the Household dealt with them.

"Money!" Zaza murmured to herself.

Then she gave a little cry.

"I know where the Master of the Household keeps money with which he pays the wages—in the safe."

"But you can hardly steal it from there."

"I think I can!"

Rachel looked at her wide-eyed.

"I have an idea...a very clever idea!" Zaza declared.

"What is it?"

"I will tell you if it is successful. If not, we will have to think of something else. What is the time?"

She looked at the clock as she spoke and saw that it was nearly four o'clock.

"I had better go and see Count Courland now. Otherwise he may be with Papa."

Zaza jumped up and went towards the door.

"Good luck!" Rachel cried.

Zaza merely smiled at her sister before she left the room.

She ran down the passages and down the stairs to the Master of the Household's very imposing office filled with huge pieces of heavy mahogany furniture and a number of tin boxes inscribed with the Royal coat-of-arms.

As she expected, Count Courland, who was a heavily built, austere-looking man, was working at his desk.

He looked up when Zaza entered, then rose to his feet slowly and with obvious reluctance.

Zaza smiled at him beguilingly.

"I am so sorry to disturb you, Count," she said, "but I wonder if I could look at the jewellery in the safe. I am choosing a new gown and I think it is important that the colour should be a background either for the sapphires or for the emeralds. I cannot decide which."

The Master of the Household made no reply, he merely took the key from the drawer of his desk and walked towards the huge safe which stood in the corner of his office.

Here there were shelves containing documents and papers, other shelves on which reposed the personal jewellery of the Royal Family, and below them, as Zaza had seen on other occasions, was a shelf containing bags of money and stacks of notes.

As soon as the Count had the door of the safe open Zaza produced several pieces of material and turned them over in her hands.

"I wonder which would be the most becoming?" she asked, as if she spoke to herself and was in no hurry to make a decision.

"Perhaps Your Royal Highness would be gracious enough to allow me to return to my work while you make up you mind?" Count Courland suggested.

"But of course, Count, and I will not be any longer than I can help," Zaza replied.

She had counted on his resenting her taking up so much of his time when he was busy.

When he had sat down again at his desk, she stood for some minutes without moving, still looking at the materials, holding first one piece, then another, up to the light.

When the Count was obviously absorbed poring over a ledger, she moved close to the safe and opened one of the jewel-boxes.

It was a large one covered in black velvet which contained a suite of sapphires. They had been one of her mother's favourite jewels and had looked magnificent in her fair hair and against her pink and white complexion.

Zaza's hair was the same colour and she thought that it would seem reasonable that she should choose those gems rather than the emeralds, which her father had always said were too flashy for a young girl.

She lifted the tiara out of the box, then the necklace and the two bracelets which matched it.

She knew the tiara was too large to fit into any other box and she put it right at the back of the shelf behind a number of jewel-boxes where it could not be seen unless they were moved.

Then she quickly put the bracelets, the brooch, the ear-rings, and the necklace into other boxes into which they would fit.

A box that contained the opals, which Zaza had never liked and thought unlucky, took most of them, and what was left over she managed to squeeze in with the topazes.

She glanced over her shoulder.

The Count was still taking no interest in her and quickly she filled the empty box with money from the shelf below.

She was careful to take notes which were in the highest denominations and added one bag of coins so that she would have some cash with her.

Then she closed the lid of the box and walked towards the Count.

This was the dangerous moment and if it was discovered what she was doing she was not certain what would happen.

She reached his desk and again with slow reluctance he rose to his feet.

"I am afraid I have been unable to decide, Count, what material would look best with Mama's sapphires, and I hope you will not mind if I take them upstairs and ask Rachel to help me, and the Countess Glucksburg. If she is not well enough this evening, I am sure she will be better tomorrow."

"Yes, yes, I heard that she was indisposed," the Count said.

"The sapphires will be quite safe tonight because I will lock them up in my bureau and you will have them back tomorrow morning."

"That is quite all right, Your Highness," Count Courland replied.

He was barely listening to Zaza, for his eyes were on his ledger and she had the feeling that he was still counting the rows of figures.

"Thank you very much, Count, you have been most kind."

The Count bowed his head perfunctorily and Zaza went from the room.

Only as she got outside the door did she give a deep sigh of relief and satisfaction.

Rachel could hardly believe that she had been so clever when she showed her the money she had taken from the safe.

"Papa will be horrified when he hears!" she said apprehensively.

"Perhaps the Count will not tell him. I am sure Papa would think it extremely remiss of him not to have watched me all the time I was at the safe and at least see exactly what I was taking away with me."

The two sisters laughed, then Rachel asked:

"What is the next thing?"

"Clothes, of course!" Zaza replied. "I can hardly ask one of the footmen to carry down a trunk and load it onto a carriage which will take me to the station."

"Can you see the servants' faces if you said anything like that?" Rachel said, laughing.

"I suppose I shall have to be content merely with what I am wearing and anything I can carry myself," Zaza said, "but at least I have some money with which to buy gowns in Paris. Think, Rachel, how exciting that will be! I am sick of all the dressmakers who come here and make clucking noises with their tongues every time I suggest anything unusual."

"I wish I could come with you," Rachel said wistfully.

"I too wish you could, dearest," Zaza answered, "and I feel very mean leaving you to face the row there will be. But you must just pretend you know nothing. It would be fatal to let Papa think we conspired together."

"Yes, of course," Rachel said, "but I shall miss you. I shall miss you desperately!"

"I do not suppose I shall be gone for long," Zaza replied, "only until my money gives out."

"But . . . suppose you never come back?"

"I think it would be impossible to stay away forever, but perhaps . . . I do not know . . . things might seem different when I get away from Melhausen and see them, so to speak, in their proper perspective."

"I understand what you are saying," Rachel said. "At the same time, how can you live in Paris all alone? You will either have to get married to somebody who does not know who you are, or . . ."

"I am not going to think about the future," Zaza interrupted, "I just want to escape and find out what the world is like outside what the Professor calls my 'painted prison.'"

"I think that is a very good name for it," Rachel said. "I have often thought it is pretty and ornamental, and the people who gape at it from the out-

side think how lucky we are, we Princesses, walking
about with crowns on our heads and everyone
curtseying to us. They do not know it is like eating
dry bread day after day with no variation in the
menu."

Zaza sat down on the bed and laughed.

"Oh, Rachel, I do love you! You always say such
funny things, and that is perfectly true. It is exactly
what we do—eat dry bread until our minds and our
stomachs are sick of it."

She laughed again before she said:

"I am expecting *haute cuisine* in Paris, cream
and truffles, champagne and oysters."

"You will have to get someone to pay for it,"
Rachel said practically, "or you will spend all your
money and be back within days!"

"I am only speaking figuratively," Zaza said,
"but you must admit it will be a very exciting adventure."

"Very, very exciting," Rachel agreed, but her
voice was wistful and Zaza knew that once again
she was thinking that she must be left behind.

Now, as the train began to speed up and she
looked round at the other occupants of the carriage,
she saw the Professor take off his tall hat and mop
his brow with his handkerchief and knew he had
been as apprehensive as she was.

She had with difficulty dressed herself in clothes
that would ensure her not being recognised the moment she left the Palace.

She put on her plainest gown with a thin summer
coat which was quite ordinary. Then she removed
all the decorations from her straw hat, leaving only
some blue ribbons which might have been worn by
any Bourgeoise in the streets of Melhausen.

She had already the night before packed everything that was possible for her to carry in a carpet-
bag which she had found in one of the box-rooms
on the School-Room landing.

It was worn and dusty and not at all the smart
luggage with which her mother had always travelled.
Zaza thought it must have belonged to one of their

Governesses who had left it behind because it was too shabby for her to use.

She managed to cram into it quite a considerable number of things and it was a relief to know that as it was summer her light gowns took up little room so that she could take several more with her than she would otherwise have been able to do.

At the same time, she kept testing the bag to be quite certain she could carry it.

The one advantage of leaving so early would be, she knew, that the senior servants in the Palace would not yet be about.

If she left as she intended before six o'clock, she would be likely to encounter only the lower maids on the stairs, who would ask no questions, and perhaps some of the under-servants who did the odd jobs, if she went out through a back door.

At the same time, never having fended for herself, the mere fact of going down the stairs to the lower parts of the Palace and leaving by a side entrance was to enter territory she had never explored before.

She lay awake for a long time anticipating innumerable difficulties and obstacles, then found that even they were easier than she had expected.

In the lower part of the Palace when she passed servants in the passages they hardly glanced at her as they moved along yawning and carrying brushes and buckets.

Then she went out a side door and into a yard which was filled with empty bottles and boxes which she had no idea even existed.

There it was easy to find a narrow road that passed along the back of the Palace and which she guessed was used only by tradesmen.

There were two sentries at the gate where it ended, but they were talking to each other and after a perfunctory glance at Zaza they did not look at her again.

Before she reached the main roadway and was out of sight of the sentries her arm was aching from the heaviness of her carpet-bag, and it was with relief that she saw a hackney-carriage that was obviously for hire.

She waved, and before the man pulled his horses to a standstill he asked:

"Where do you want to go? I'm on my way home."

"Please, will you take me to the station?" Zaza asked.

She thought he was about to refuse, and added pleadingly:

"I have a train to catch and if I miss it I shall get into a great deal of trouble."

"All right then," the cabby said in a surly tone. "Get in!"

He made no attempt to help her with her baggage and Zaza thought with a little smile that it was very different from the way she was usually treated.

Once she was in, the cabby whipped up his tired horse and she thought with satisfaction that she was being carried away from the Palace and there was unlikely to be a hue and cry after her for at least several hours.

She arrived at the station to find, to her relief, that the Professor was waiting outside the main entrance as he had promised to do.

She was not certain if he was relieved to see her or if he was in fact rather horrified at the idea of what they were doing.

Anyway, there was no time for conversation.

He paid the hackney-carriage and took her bag from her. She waited while he bought their tickets at the Booking-Office, then they walked together onto the platform.

For a moment Zaza was afraid that someone might recognise her, but she told herself that the people who took an early-morning train to Paris were not likely to expect to see their Princess alone with an elderly man.

Nevertheless, it was hard to wait until the train puffed slowly into the station.

Now there was no red carpet, no attendants, no Aides-de-Camp to usher them into the Royal

Carriage, no stewards to bring them refreshments, no fussing Ladys-in-Waiting to help Zaza off with her coat.

There was only the Professor, already deeply engrossed in the morning newspapers.

'I have done it!' Zaza thought to herself, and longed to shout out loud: "I have done it, I have escaped! I am on my way to Paris!"

Chapter Two

The journey to Paris took five hours, and when Zaza saw the other passengers in the carriage opening luncheon-baskets and boxes, she realised that she should have brought some food with her.

Of course the Professor, whose mind was always on something else, had not thought of anything so material as food, and as the hours passed she began to feel very hungry.

It had been impossible for her to have anything to eat before she left the Palace, and she found herself thinking of the fragrant hot coffee which Rachel would be enjoying and the many breakfast-dishes that she would be offered, besides the *croissants* warm from the oven which the Chef baked every day.

The Grand-Duke liked a combination of French and German dishes for his meals, as if even in this particular he united the separate nationalities of his subjects.

The result was that Zaza had found there was always too much to eat and she and her mother had often sat looking wide-eyed at the amount of food that her father and the Courtiers could consume apparently without feeling over-fed.

But now with the excitement of her escape she felt both hungry and thirsty, and as the train stopped at what she knew was a large town she asked the Professor tentatively:

"Would it be possible to buy some food here?"

"Food?" he exclaimed as if he had never heard of the substance.

"I am hungry," Zaza said with a smile.

"How could I have been so foolish, so remiss, not to have brought something with us," he said, putting his hand up to his forehead as if he rebuked himself.

"Perhaps there will be something we can buy at the station," Zaza suggested.

"Of course, of course," he agreed.

As the train came to a standstill he put his hat down on the seat next to Zaza as if to prevent anyone else from occupying it and sprang onto the platform.

She thought as she watched him walk away in search of food that she would be more likely to have to look after him than he to look after her.

She knew of old how absent-minded he was, and yet he was so kindly that she really had no qualms about trusting herself to him, knowing that if need be he would die for her, although he might find it more difficult to live with her.

Most of the passengers in the carriage were, she thought, commercial travellers or perhaps shop-keepers travelling to Paris in search of new wares.

Everything that was at all attractive in Melhausen, especially in Dorné, the Capital, came from Paris.

This upset the German citizens who frequently complained that they were not catered for and their wishes were never considered.

At the same time, Zaza had always felt that the Melhausians modified the elegance and the originality of what was French until they took away its *chic* and in their hands everything became slightly dowdy and ordinary.

Now she would see for herself what was really French.

She felt almost like singing with excitement. At the same time, she knew they still had to cross the border and that might be a dangerous moment.

Their passports would be inspected and, what

was more, if her disappearance from the Palace had
been discovered her father might telegraph the
guards to stop and question anybody who looked at
all like her and was of the same age.

She knew, however, that she was frightening
herself unnecessarily.

The first person to discover that she was not in
her room would be her personal maid, who would
call her as usual at eight o'clock.

If she was not there, Elenmore would suppose
her to be with her sister, Rachel. She would doubtless
lay out the gown she was to wear today and wait
patiently for her to return so that she could help
her-dress.

Zaza had been careful to leave nothing which
might indicate that she had left the Palace.

She had put the note for her father not in her
bedroom but on a table in the passage where she
thought it was unlikely anyone would notice it for
some hours, if then.

"When they ask you where I am," she instructed
Rachel, "say vaguely that you think I had an early
music-lesson, or I might be with Papa. You know
that no-one on the School-Room floor would bother
to go as far as the Music-Room, and they would
certainly not intrude upon Papa."

"You are thinking of everything," Rachel said
admiringly. "I have never known you to be so practical."

"I have never before wanted to do anything so
outrageous as to escape from the Palace," Zaza said
with a laugh. "But you know how Mama used to
say, 'If a thing is worth doing, it is worth doing
well'? Well, that certainly applies to this adventure."

"Of course," Rachel said. "It would be very ig-
nominious to be dragged home even before you reach
Paris."

"That is what I think," Zaza agreed.

They talked until Zaza thought it was too late
for Rachel to still be awake.

Before she left her sister she said:

"One thing I am determined to do in Paris is to

find out if there is anything that will help you to get better. I have always heard that Parisian Doctors and French medicaments are very much in advance of those of other countries in Europe, and I am sure that in Melhausen we are behind everybody."

Rachel's eyes seemed to light up in her pale little face.

"If you have time to think of me, Zaza," she said, "that would be a wonderful thing to do."

"Of course I shall think about you," Zaza said. "How can I do anything else? I wish I could write to you, but it might be dangerous."

"Can you imagine what Papa would say if I received a postcard of the Eiffel Tower!" Rachel exclaimed, and they both giggled at the idea of how furious the Grand-Duke would be.

Looking out the window of the train, Zaza saw the Professor coming back towards the carriage, carrying her food.

In one hand he had a plate on which she saw a French roll split in half with a large slice of ham in the middle, and two *pâtisseries* filled with cream.

In the other hand he carried a thick china mug filled with coffee.

Zaza opened the door for him, exclaiming as she did so:

"That looks delicious!"

"You will have to drink the cup of coffee quickly as I have to return the cup and the plate," he said. "They made me leave a deposit on it."

Zaza's eyes twinkled.

It was amusing to think that he might be suspected of trying to steal the cup and plate, and she wondered what the suspicious attendant would say if he knew that what the Professor had bought was in reality for the Princess Marie-Celeste.

However, she was too hungry even to joke about it in a whisper to the Professor, and as she ate the sandwich she found the crisp fresh bread delicious.

"Have you had something to eat too?" she asked the Professor as she finished the last crumb.

"I did not think of it," he answered.

"How can you be so stupid?" she asked. "You will be very hungry before we reach Paris."

"Yes, yes, of course," he agreed.

He pulled out his watch, saw the time, and said:

"I have time to get myself something when I return the china."

Zaza quickly gulped down the coffee.

"Take it now," she said, "and get yourself a ham-roll like the one I have just eaten. It was delicious!"

He hurried away and she told herself that when they reached Paris she would have to be very firm with him in seeing that he ate at regular hours.

'He is getting old,' she thought, 'and he does not look very well.'

It struck her that his face was very lined and he was also pale and had a somewhat unhealthy pallor.

"What would I do if I lost the Professor?" she asked herself.

She knew that if that happened there would be no-one to talk to in the Palace and she would be left having orders barked at her by her father, or listening to the eternal strictures of the Countess Glucksburg.

She began to be afraid in case the Professor forgot the time and missed the train.

It suddenly struck her that she had never asked him where they would be staying in Paris and if she arrived alone in the Capital she might never find him again.

She began to feel a sense of panic because the porters were shutting the doors of the carriages and she could see the guard moving along the platform with a red flag in his hand.

Then just as she was becoming frantic she saw the Professor hurrying towards the carriage and she opened the door for him.

"I was beginning to worry," she said almost

breathlessly. "You were so long and the train might have gone without you."

"The woman was an unconscionable time giving me my change," the Professor explained.

He had hardly shut the door and sat down in his seat before there was a whistle, the guard waved his flag, and the train started to move.

This was certainly very different, Zaza thought, from travelling in the Royal manner, when the train left when her father was ready for it to do so, and not before.

She was extremely relieved to have the Professor back beside her and she smiled at him but did not speak again of her fears in case he might think she was finding fault.

They reached the last station in Melhausen and now Zaza looked out the window to see a number of soldiers on the platform wearing the green uniform her father thought was very smart and to which he kept adding different improvements.

"This is where we cross the border," she said to the Professor, and her voice shook a little as the idea made her nervous.

The Professor put his hand in his pocket and drew out the passport which she knew belonged to his niece.

It took the form of a letter written by the Secretary of State for Home Affairs, and it instructed those whom it concerned to give every possible help and protection to Gabrielle Dumont, who was a citizen of the Royal Duchy of Melhausen.

Zaza read it carefully and had it in her hand as the soldiers opened the door.

It was a young officer who came to their carriage and he took Zaza's passport first, opened it, and then glanced at her.

There was no doubt that what he saw pleased him, and he continued looking and with a little bow handed back the passport without really reading it.

"*Merci, Monsieur,*" Zaza said.

"You are going to Paris, *M'mselle?*"

"*Oui, Monsieur.*"

"Then I hope you have a very pleasant journey."

"Thank you, *Monsieur*."

The officer looked at the Professor's passport, then passed down the centre of the carriage to inspect those belonging to the other occupants.

He kept glancing back at Zaza and it was quite obvious that he was interested in no-one else.

As he left he smiled at her, and when she smiled back he saluted her before he moved farther down the platform.

She thought it was the first time in her life that a young man had treated her as an ordinary girl rather than as a Royal Princess and it was exciting to know that she was admired just for herself.

Before the train proceeded, the officer passed the carriage again, and although Zaza knew he was waiting to catch her eye, she did not glance in his direction but looked demurely at the Professor's newspaper which she had on her lap.

Only as the train finally moved on did she have an impulse to get up and lean out the window.

As she had half-suspected, the officer was almost at the end of the platform, and as she passed him he saluted her again and this time she waved her hand.

A smile illuminated his face and as she sat down again Zaza felt she had been very daring.

'How shocked everyone would be if they knew what I was doing,' she thought.

She was sure the Countess Glucksburg would swoon away at the impropriety of it.

Slowly, because it was uphill, the train puffed over the frontier and they were in France.

'I have escaped!' Zaza thought. 'I am free!' She wanted to cry aloud with excitement.

There were three hours more to travel before they could reach Paris and Zaza had the idea that the train was running late.

However, there was so much to see from the windows that now she was not in such a hurry to reach Paris.

They passed through the mountains and the tree-covered country on the border, then came down onto fertile agricultural land. She could see the peasants toiling in the hedgeless fields, some of them driving white bullocks, others using horses, and many with no assistance except their own muscles.

There were little hamlets and many Churches with their spires pointing towards the sky.

It was all exactly as her picture-books had told her it should be and Zaza was entranced by everything she saw.

There were also long waits at small and large stations and once again the Professor procured some food and Zaza thought that once they were alone she should tell him that she had brought plenty of money with her and she would pay him back for everything he had expended on her behalf.

"I must be very careful with my money," she told herself, "because if it were stolen I would not be able to get any more."

She had a vague idea that most people did not travel with large sums of cash upon them. They had letters of credit.

She wanted to ask the Professor what he was doing about money, but it was impossible while there were other people in the carriage.

Only when they were halfway to Paris did three of their fellow-travellers leave the carriage and now there was only one old man left in the far corner and he was sleeping peacefully.

At last Zaza could talk, and, speaking with her face near to the Professor's ear, she said:

"Tell me what we are going to do when we reach Paris."

"I sent a telegram last night to my friends saying I would be arriving today and bringing somebody with me," he said. "They will get us rooms in the Hotel where they meet, which is the Café at the end of the Rue St. Honoré."

"Why do they meet at a Café?" Zara enquired.

"To talk, to discuss, to make plans," the Professor replied. "We have a Club and we call ourselves *La Révolte des Coeurs*."

"The Revolt of Hearts," Zaza said. "That sounds a very good name."

"We speak from our hearts, we feel with our hearts, and we fight with our hearts," the Professor said with satisfaction.

"Do you think your friends will allow me to join you?"

"Of course! They will accept anyone I introduce," the Professor replied. "But remember, they will think you are my niece."

"Yes," Zaza said. "I must not forget that, and I must call you Uncle François."

"I shall be very proud and honoured for you to do so," the Professor said.

His eyes lit up as he said:

"We will find freedom! Freedom even for a woman! And now at last you will understand what I have been trying to explain to you for so long."

He spoke in an ecstatic tone which told Zaza that he was carried away by his own words, and she sat back listening to him, feeling that she was moving in an exciting dream.

She was half-afraid she might wake up to find herself in bed at the Palace, with nothing to look forward to except the hours she would spend in the Music-Room with the Professor and their conversations when the Countess was asleep.

There were more scenes to watch from the window, then the Professor began to gather together some papers he had been reading and put them in one of the cases which he carried.

"We are not far from Paris," he said. "I wonder if one of my friends will meet me. I think it unlikely. They will be waiting for me at the Café des Champs and, I am quite certain, waiting impatiently."

He stood up to lift down from the rack their other luggage, including, Zaza noticed, his violin.

As he did so there was a sudden crash, the carriage swayed and shook, and the Professor fell down to the floor while the luggage from the racks toppled over on top of him.

Zaza gave a scream.

She was flung forward violently in her seat, but she managed to save herself from falling to the floor, and as she realised there had been a collision she heard the Professor groan.

There was the noise of escaping steam outside, men's voices shouting, and the shrill screaming of a woman.

Then as the carriage seemed to settle itself again, Zaza stood up and pulled the luggage off the Professor.

"Are you all right?" she asked. "You are not hurt?"

She lifted the boxes he had brought with him, her own carpet-bag, and his violin onto the seats, then as she put out her hands to help him rise, he gave another groan.

"You are hurt!" she exclaimed.

"It is my ankle," he replied. "I twisted it as I fell."

"You do not think it is broken?"

"No, no. It is not broken," the Professor said almost testily, "but it is very painful. Help me onto the seat."

The old man in the corner who had been asleep was saying in an angry voice in German:

"It is disgraceful! These accidents should not happen! It is typical of the incompetence of the French, who cannot even run a railway-line safely."

Neither the Professor nor Zaza took any notice.

Carefully, because she knew he was in pain, she helped support the Professor onto the seat and he sat with his leg stuck out in front of him. She wondered if he ought to take off his laced boot.

He was looking dusty, his hat was battered, and she thought if only he had not been standing up when the collision occurred he would not have been hurt.

But it was too late for regrets.

"Are you all right?" she asked.

She thought he looked very pale and he seemed, for him, unusually silent.

He put his hand to his heart and said in a voice that was little above a whisper:

"Look in my pocket. There is a bottle. If you will give me two or three drops from it, I shall be all right."

Frantically Zaza felt in his pocket and found the bottle as he had said.

She was about to hand it to him but then thought that at the moment he looked too weak even to take it from her.

She found when she pulled the top off that it contained a dropper. Squeezing a little of the liquid into it, she said:

"Will you open your mouth?"

The Professor did as he was told and she put several drops of it onto his tongue.

"Is that enough?" she asked.

He obviously could not speak, but he nodded his head and she sat down on the seat next to him, watching him anxiously as the colour came back into his cheeks.

Several minutes elapsed while the German at the other end of the carriage was still grumbling and complaining. Now he was leaning out the window, shouting at those who were hurrying up the line, asking them what had occurred.

"Do you feel better?" Zaza asked the Professor.

"A little," he replied in a normal voice. "It is just that I have had trouble with my heart lately. But as long as I have the drops with me I am all right."

Zaza gave a sigh of relief.

She slipped the bottle back into the Professor's pocket, then rose to go to the window on their side of the carriage.

"I must see what is happening," she said.

She looked out to see that at the front of the train there were a great number of people all talking and gesticulating, while the steam which filled the air with its noise was obviously made not by one engine but two.

"I think there has been a collision between two trains," she said to the Professor.

"I imagined that was what had occurred," he replied.

Now Zaza could see an official and several other men coming down the train, stopping at every carriage to ask if its occupants were all right.

She waited until they reached hers, then she said:

"There is a gentleman here who has injured his leg. I wonder if there is a Doctor who could attend to him."

The official in uniform glanced back as if he thought there was a Doctor amongst the crowd by the engines.

Then a man dressed in ordinary clothes said:

"Let me see what I can do."

As he spoke he looked at Zaza and she had the feeling that, like the officer at the previous station, he found her attractive and was therefore willing to offer his assistance.

Because she was so glad of anyone who would help, she smiled at him as he climbed up into the carriage.

As he entered it he seemed to be much taller than he had looked on the ground, and as she thought it was a good thing to appear helpless, she merely said, indicating the Professor:

"This is my uncle, and I am afraid he may have broken his ankle. That is why I would like a Doctor to see him."

"I think it is only twisted," the Professor said sharply.

"Nevertheless, I am sure it is very painful, *Monsieur*," the young man said.

"That is true," the Professor agreed.

He tried to move his leg and winced, and Zaza said quickly:

"Do not move!"

She looked at the man who had come to help them and asked:

"What can we do? How can we get to Paris from here?"

"Actually you are already in Paris," the young man answered, "and the best thing would be for me to find you a *voiture* which will carry you to where you wish to go."

"Will you do that?" Zaza asked. "It would certainly be very kind."

"I am sure it can be managed," the young man replied. "Wait here and leave everything to me."

As he spoke he was looking at her in a manner which told her that he would certainly exert himself on her behalf, and she wished she could tell Rachel of her success with men now that she was away from the restrictions of the Palace.

The young man climbed down onto the railway-line and Zaza rose to shut the door behind him.

Then as she leant out the window he said:

"Perhaps before I leave you it might be a good idea to know your name. Mine is Pierre Beauvais."

"My uncle is Professor Dumont," Zaza replied.

"And yours?"

It was quite obvious that that was what he wanted to know, and Zaza said with a little smile:

"My name is Zaza Dumont."

"Thank you, *Mademoiselle*," Pierre Beauvais said. "I will be as quick as I can in procuring a *voiture*, but I suspect there will be quite a number of people on the train with the same idea."

"I can only rely on you, *Monsieur*," Zaza answered.

He smiled at her, and as he walked away she realised that while he was dressed in an unusual fashion he had no hat, and she wondered if it had been damaged or lost in the collision.

She also saw that his clothes were what she would have expected an artist in Paris might wear, but they were certainly not those of a gentleman, at any rate not the sort that she met at the Palace.

'Perhaps he is an Impressionist,' she thought, and knew how exciting it would be to meet one after she had heard so much about them from the Professor.

Thinking of the Professor, she turned dutifully to sit down beside him.

"That kind young man, *Monsieur* Pierre Beauvais, has gone to find a *voiture* to carry us into Paris," she said. "I am afraid it may be somewhat expensive, but do not worry. I have quite a lot of money with me."

She spoke in a low voice, but there was actually no chance of anyone overhearing them because the German had climbed out on the other side of the carriage and was airing his grievances to anyone who would listen.

"That was sensible of you," the Professor replied, "but I think I have enough for both of us."

"I cannot allow you to spend your money on me," Zaza said, "and when you are feeling better I will tell you how clever I was to obtain the money I required without anyone in the Palace being aware of it."

"My foot will be all right by tomorrow," the Professor said in a reassuring tone. "I cannot be ill or incapacitated now at this moment when I am in Paris and with you, *ma Princesse*."

"Hush!"

Zaza put up her fingers and laid them on his lips.

"You must never say that again. It is dangerous. I am your niece, Gabrielle, remember? And because I shall find it difficult to remember a new name, you must call me Zaza as Rachel always does."

"Zaza," the Professor repeated as if he were a child.

"Zaza Dumont. I think it sounds rather nice," Zaza said with a smile. "Let me say I am very proud and very honoured to be your niece, and I only hope I shall do you credit."

"It is I who have the honour," the Professor said.

There was a note in his voice that told Zaza he was very moved by her words.

"To have you with me," he went on, "and to be in Paris is like reaching El Dorado when for so many years it has only been a mirage on the horizon of my thoughts."

He took her hand as he spoke and kissed it.

"My best, my most brilliant, my most promising pupil," he said. "Paris, the City of learning, of culture, and of freedom, lies ahead of us."

*   *   *

Driving in the ancient *voiture* with the Professor beside her and Pierre Beauvais sitting on the small seat opposite, Zaza thought it was difficult not to feel shy when a man's eyes shone with an unconcealed admiration she had never seen before.

But she was so grateful to *Monsieur* Beauvais and so glad that he had been there to manage everything that she would not have been able to resent anything he said or did, because without him it would have been impossible for her to cope.

He and another man had carried the Professor from the carriage quite a long distance to the road where the *voiture* was waiting for them.

A third man had brought their luggage.

Zaza had wondered whether she ought to tip him, but she was afraid of doing the wrong thing and also had no idea exactly how much she should give, until she had seen Pierre Beauvais do it for her.

She told herself she must somehow make it up to him, although she was not quite certain how.

Now, when they were free of the numerous carriages which had been procured for other travellers, Pierre Beauvais leant forward to say to the Professor:

"You will forgive me for being curious, *Monsieur*, but when you gave your address as the Hôtel des Champs I wondered if in fact you had any particular reason for staying there."

The Professor, who had been looking rather grave because, as Zaza knew, he was in pain, looked up sharply and replied:

"Why should you be interested?"

Pierre Beauvais seemed to hesitate before, obviously choosing his words, he said:

"I myself am rather anxious to meet those who gather at the Café des Champs."

The Professor seemed suddenly alert and Zaza thought he was taking in the appearance of their rescuer for the first time.

He looked at the young man sitting opposite him wearing a velvet coat, plain black trousers, and a floppy bow-tie, and now, although he had not put it on, Zaza saw that beside him on the small seat was a large-brimmed black felt hat.

"You have friends who patronise the Café des Champs?" the Professor enquired.

"Shall I say that I have heard about it," Pierre Beauvais answered. "And I am very anxious to meet the members of the *Révolte des Coeurs*."

The Professor gave a cry of delight.

"You are a Symbolist!" he exclaimed. "I might have guessed it from your appearance. Surely it must be fate that you should have rescued us."

He held out his hand as he spoke, and as Pierre Beauvais took it, the Professor said:

"Welcome, my son! Welcome to a band of men who fight for freedom of the mind and freedom of the soul!"

"I am delighted to meet you, *Monsieur*," Pierre Beauvais said. "I was hoping so much that having come to Paris I would not be turned away by *les Coeurs*."

"They will certainly not do that when they know you are a friend of mine," the Professor replied. "They will welcome you for the Samaritan you are and because your ideals are my ideals and of course those of my niece—Zaza."

There was a pause before he said her name, and Zaza knew that in his usual absent-minded fashion he had for the moment forgotten it.

"Is *Mademoiselle* also a Symbolist?" Pierre Beauvais asked in a tone of surprise.

"I wish to become one," Zaza said quickly before the Professor could speak.

But he would not be circumvented in what he wished to say.

"This child is my most brilliant pupil," he said to Pierre Beauvais. "She is sensible, perceptive, and very brave. She is a woman but that shall not prevent her from coming into contact with brains that are the equal of her own."

Pierre Beauvais looked at Zaza in a way that told her he thought it was unnecessary for her to be clever because she was beautiful.

She wanted to surprise him with her intelligence, but for the moment she felt a little shy and was unable to meet his eyes.

They drove on, and now the Professor, forgetting the pain of his injury, was holding forth on the familiar theme of freedom from the Bourgeoisie, of a new Constitution in which men of intelligence would have preference over those who were against all progress or deviation from the traditional.

"What we need, my confederates tell me," the Professor boomed, "is something different from the middle-class life reflected in the paintings of Renoir and Degas."

Zaza turned to look at him in surprise because she had thought he admired the Impressionists for striking out in a new manner which at least was a rebellion against the conservative art which filled the Academy and the Salons.

"We are also," the Professor continued, "not concerned with bawdy gaiety, which that ridiculous creature Toulouse Lautrec depicts so vulgarly."

"Then what do we want?" Pierre Beauvais enquired.

"We want a new world; a world where man can rise to the heights within himself and be accepted not for the money he earns but for the greatness that lies within his soul."

Zaza thought with a little hint of amusement that Pierre Beauvais looked surprised by the manner

in which the Professor was speaking as well as by
what he said.

She was so used to his proclaiming that it was
not unusual to her, but she could understand that
the young man opposite found it somewhat extraordinary.

Again she was thinking how lucky it was that
he had been there to rescue them. She liked the
manner in which he had arranged some of their
luggage so that it supported the Professor's injured
foot and made him comparatively comfortable in the
voiture.

"You have somewhere to stay in Paris?" the
Professor asked as if he suddenly descended from
the heights down into the valley of the commonplace.

"Like you, I have only just arrived," Pierre Beauvais said with a smile. "When I have left you at
the Hôtel des Champs I will look for somewhere to
lay my head."

The Professor made a gesture with his hand.

"Why not the Hôtel des Champs?" he enquired.
"It is not *de luxe*—there is no need for me to tell
you that—but it is clean and the food is good. Need
I say more?"

"I would not wish to impose upon you, *Monsieur*," Pierre Beauvais replied.

"It is no imposition, for you are one of us. We
are brothers—brothers under the skin—and what else
matters?"

"If you would be kind enough to introduce me
to the Hotel as well as to the members of *La
Révolte des Coeurs*," Pierre Beauvais said, "I shall
be eternally in your debt."

He was speaking to the Professor, but as he
spoke he was looking at Zaza and she had the feeling
that he would stay anywhere and do anything so
long as she was there.

Unpacking in a very small bedroom which overlooked the Rue St. Honoré, Zaza thought she had
never felt so excited or so alive.

Perhaps it was the Professor's enthusiasm and

the air of the City, which she had always longed
to breathe, or perhaps it was the fact that Pierre
Beauvais was with them and she was no longer
afraid that she would have to look after the Professor
all by herself.

He seemed in an unobtrusive but efficient manner to have taken charge of them from the moment
they had arrived at the Hôtel des Champs.

It was a small, narrow, upright building, with
the inevitable grey shutters and somewhat closed appearance like the other houses of Paris, which looked,
Zaza thought, like lovely women with their eyes shut.

Leaving them in the carriage, Pierre Beauvais
had gone in search of the Concierge, who had
helped him carry the Professor up the stairs to his
room on the third floor.

It was sparsely furnished but, as the Professor
had said, it was clean and the bed looked comfortable.

"What I suggest you do, *Mademoiselle*," Pierre
Beauvais said, "is to unpack your own things while
I get the Professor into bed. Then I will find the
name of a Doctor from the Proprietor and either
fetch him or send for him to call as soon as possible."

"Are you quite certain you can manage?" Zaza
asked somewhat helplessly.

She had begun to think it might be very difficult
for her as well as embarrassing if she had to help
the Professor undress.

She was quite certain that if she even suggested
such a thing he would remember her Royal rank
and violently resist her doing anything to help him,
in which case the people in the Hotel might think
it very strange.

Pierre Beauvais got his way and she went to her
own room, which was on the other side of the corridor, and started to unpack her carpet-bag.

Never having packed for herself before, she had
not made a very good job of it the previous night
and she shook out her gowns rather ruefully, seeing
that some of them were very creased.

She was also quite certain that there must have been a dozen things she had forgotten, and it was a relief to find at the bottom of her bag the large number of notes which she had stolen from the safe.

The coins were in her purse and she thought she must find out from Pierre Beauvais what he had paid for the *voiture* that had brought them from the train and pay him back for that and for what he had tipped the porter.

She thought it was really ridiculous to have been brought up never to handle money, not to know how much to pay for things, how much to tip, or how much she should carry about with her.

If she left the money in her bedroom it might be stolen, and although she intended to discuss all this with the Professor, she thought perhaps now was not the right moment to do so, when he was upset and in pain.

She had finished her unpacking and was wondering what she should do next when there was a knock on the door.

"Who is it?" she asked.

"It is I, Pierre Beauvais."

Quickly she opened the door.

"The Professor is comfortable and in bed," he said, "and I have sent for the Doctor. I do not know how soon he will come, but I do not think your uncle's ankle is broken, although it is swollen."

"How can you tell?"

"To be honest, I have no medical experience, but I have seen fractures and breaks and I am almost certain in your uncle's case his leg has been no more than severely strained. It should soon be all right with cold-water bandages and, of course, rest."

"He will be so disappointed that he cannot see his friends."

"Surely if they meet here they will come up to his room."

Zaza gave a little exclamation.

"Of course! Why did I not think of that? Perhaps

you could contact them. The Proprietor or some-body will know who and where they are."

"Leave it to me," Pierre Beauvais said.

He spoke in a manner which, Zaza thought, made her only too willing to leave everything to him.

"I want to thank you for all you have done for us," she said, "and please . . . may I give you back the money you spent in paying for the *voiture* and in tipping the porter?"

To her annoyance, she blushed as she spoke and felt ridiculously shy.

It was absurd, she knew, but she had never before had to discuss money with a man and she felt that it was embarrassing, although why it should be she had no idea.

To her surprise, Pierre Beauvais seemed embar-rassed too.

"That is all right," he said.

"But I cannot allow you to pay for us . . . and my uncle would not like it either," Zaza said.

She paused for a moment, then she said:

"It is no use pretending that you are well off when you are staying here in this cheap Hotel."

"I am not pretending anything of the sort," Pierre Beauvais replied. "And surely this is something I can discuss with your uncle when he is well enough."

Too late Zaza realised that if she really had been the Professor's niece she would have left financial matters to him and it would have been very unlikely that she would have any money of her own.

Then quickly she found a way of excusing her-self.

"I know most women have little to do with money," she said, "especially when they have a man with them, but my uncle is so absent-minded that he always forgets practical matters."

She managed to give a little laugh as she went on:

"He usually forgets to eat, and when he is thinking of his music or of his Symbolism nothing else exists in the whole world."

"I can understand that," Pierre Beauvais said, "and I can see what it means to him."

"Everything!" Zaza said. "He was so excited about coming to Paris to join his friends, and it will be tragic if he has to stay in bed and cannot be with them."

"You are not to worry," Pierre Beauvais replied. "I will arrange everything. If he wants to go downstairs I will have him carried down. Perhaps that would be better than asking his friends to come to him. He will no doubt want the noise, the music, the laughter, and the chatter of the Café, and I expect too the food and the wine."

Zaza felt he painted a picture which would thrill her as much as it would thrill the Professor.

"You understand," she said, "as ... few people ... do."

She was thinking at the moment of her life at the Palace, and she started when Pierre Beauvais said:

"Why do you say it like that? Surely people find it very easy to understand you, *Mademoiselle* Zaza or at least to want to."

"It is not as easy as you think," Zaza said lightly.

"I was just wondering," Pierre said, "as we have been so long on that train and it has taken us some time to get here, whether you are as hungry as I am."

Zaza's eyes lit up.

"I am indeed," she said, "but I thought it would be right to wait for dinner."

"From all your uncle was saying just now," Pierre Beauvais said, "his friends do not meet until about nine o'clock. I understand some of them have to come a long distance and others work late."

"Nine o'clock!" Zaza exclaimed in dismay.

"What I was going to suggest," he went on, "is that you and I have something light to eat now, perhaps a glass of wine, an omelette, and a cup of coffee, and after that we will be able to wait without discomfort until your uncle and his friends all gather in the Café."

"Could we do that?" Zaza asked.

"Why not?" he enquired. "You only have to say yes to my invitation."

It struck her that it was the sort of invitation she had never had before in her life!

For the moment the idea of being alone in the company of a man she had only just met and to whom she had not even been introduced struck her as so outrageous that she almost refused to do what he suggested, simply because it was something she had never imagined might happen.

But then she told herself that she was free. She was no longer within the confines of the Palace and its protocol need not now concern her.

She made up her mind.

"Thank you very much!" she said. "I would like that, but I think first I should go and see my uncle and tell him what I am about to do."

"I will wait for you downstairs in the vestibule."

He smiled at her and walked away and Zaza felt her heart was beating fast as if at the very audacity of what she was about to do.

Then she went back to the bedroom, picked up her money, and wrapped it in a chiffon scarf, having first put several notes in her handbag.

Then she crossed the corridor, knocked on the door of the Professor's bedroom, and heard him call out: "*Entrez!*"

He was lying in bed and it gave her quite a shock to see him wearing a nightshirt.

She had never seen a man in a nightshirt before, not even her father, and she thought the Professor looked very strange without the stiff white collar and black tie in which he had habitually been dressed for the last ten years of their acquaintance.

"That this should have happened, *ma Princesse!*" the Professor said as she walked towards him. "I am humiliated by my own clumsiness. I should have moved like an athlete and not like a lump of coal!"

Zaza laughed.

"How could you have anticipated that the train would be so foolish as to run into another one? But

you need not worry. When it is time to meet your
friends, that kind *Monsieur* Beauvais will have you
carried downstairs. All you have to do now is to
rest a little and wait for the Doctor."

"Beauvais is a nice young man," the Professor
said, "and just the sort of person who should be a
Symbolist, in every meaning of the word."

"As I am hungry and thirsty," Zaza said,
"*Monsieur* Beauvais has suggested he take me somewhere where we can eat. Is there anything you would
like?"

"He suggested that to me too," the Professor
replied, "and has promised to order everything I
need. Do not worry about me. Go out and enjoy
yourself."

He gave a groan as he added:

"I wanted to show you Paris. I wanted to watch
your face and hear your thoughts when you first saw
the City of my heart. But alas, it is not to be!"

"*Monsieur* Beauvais says that in a few days you
will be all right," Zaza said, "and I am sure there will
be a great deal left for you to show me. You know
I would rather see it with you than with anybody
else in the world!"

She knew her words delighted the old man and
he reached for her hand and when she gave it to
him he kissed it.

"You and Paris are the most beautiful things I
know," he said, "so I want you to meet each other."

"Now you are being poetical," Zaza said. "Tonight I am sure there will be new poems for us to
hear, new poems that I must learn. It is very, very
exciting!"

As she spoke she walked across the room to
stand looking out the window.

It struck her how hot it was, much hotter than
it had been in Melhausen, and the trees she could
see from the window looked as if they were drooping
a little for want of water.

Even so, there was something in the air which
was as exhilarating as a sharp wind or the frost on a
cold winter's day.

"I am in Paris," she said, as if she would convince herself that she was not dreaming and had really reached her journey's end.

"Yes, Paris!" the Professor echoed from the bed. "I feel as if after being in exile far too long, I have come home."

"That is exactly what you have done," Zaza said, turning towards him. "I shall not be long. You do not mind my leaving you?"

"No, of course not," the Professor replied. "Go out and enjoy yourself. I like that young man and I am sure we can trust him."

"I am sure we can," Zaza agreed, "but perhaps it would be unwise to be too trusting, and that is why I have brought you my money to look after while I am away."

She held out the bundle wrapped in the chiffon scarf which she held in her hand.

The Professor looked at it in surprise.

"Put it under your pillow," she said, "where no-one can steal it, and I will take it away with me when I come back and find somewhere safe to put it when we go downstairs to the Café.'

"You are very sensible," the Professor said.

"I try to think what Mama would do if she were in my place," Zaza replied, "since I have always believed that the English are sensible and not as emotional as the French."

"They are frigid, cold-hearted, and completely insular!" the Professor flashed.

"While the French are emotional, impulsive, and at times very profligate," Zaza retorted.

The Professor was about to reply when she said:

"You are to rest and not argue. Keep all your *bons mots* for your friends tonight. In the meantime, sleep well!"

"You are very good to me," the Professor said, "but God is good too. He has brought us to Paris!"

Chapter Three

Sitting in the small Café, Zaza thought it was not only strange but very exciting to be alone with a man.

She had never before had a meal alone with one person, let alone an attractive young man who looked at her in a manner which made her feel shy and also tense in a way she did not understand because it was so exciting.

She felt almost as if she was waiting for something to happen, although what it was she had no idea.

She told herself it must all be part of walking into a strange world and leaving behind everything familiar and having not the least idea what would happen next.

How could she have imagined even yesterday as she had walked along the corridor towards the Music-Room without the Countess that she would run away from the Palace, be involved in a train collision, and find herself in a public Restaurant with a man to whom she had not even been formally introduced?

She felt once again that Pierre Beauvais had taken charge, because without even asking her what she would like, he ordered for them ham omelettes and a bottle of wine, and afterwards cheese and coffee.

"Your uncle tells me that the food at the Café

des Champs is good," he said, "so we will not be greedy and spoil our appetites for supper."

"I should have been very, very hungry if I had had nothing to eat before nine o'clock," Zaza replied.

She was breaking the crisp fresh roll that lay beside her plate and spreading it with butter because she was too hungry to wait until the omelette came.

"Now tell me about yourself," Pierre Beauvais said.

"I would much rather we talked about ... you."

"I would find that very dull, while you are absorbingly interesting—as well as other things."

"What other ... things?" Zaza enquired.

"Do you want me to tell you how beautiful you are?"

It was not only what he said but the way he said it that made the colour rise in her face.

She looked away from him, wondering how she could stop him from paying her compliments and at the same time wanting to hear them.

"I could hardly believe you were real," Pierre Beauvais went on, "when I saw you leaning out of the carriage asking for help."

"I was very ... worried about my ... uncle."

"I am sorry he has hurt his leg. At the same time, if he had not done so I might have passed on and had no idea there was anyone so exquisite hidden in a second-class carriage."

"You are ... making me feel ... embarrassed," Zaza protested.

He looked at her for a long moment, then he said:

"It is extraordinary that you should find my very inadequate compliments embarrassing and that they should make you shy. After all, you must have listened to them all your life."

Zaza smiled and shook her head.

He had no idea, she thought, that she had received very few compliments; for if anyone in the Palace had spoken to her as Pierre Beauvais had,

she was sure that her father would have sent two
soldiers to march him out through the front door.

"Where have you come from?" Pierre Beauvais
asked.

Zaza had not expected this question and she told
herself it was something she should have discussed
with the Professor.

Then she thought there was no point in lying.

After all, the Professor's friends would know that
he had been living in Melhausen, and there was
no reason for Pierre Beauvais to connect the Professor's niece with any more-important rank in the
Royal Duchy.

"My uncle lives in Melhausen," she replied.

"In Dorné?"

"Yes."

Zaza thought she would try to side-track Pierre
Beauvais from being interested in herself by saying:

"My uncle was once a very famous musician.
He gave recitals in Paris and in many other Capitals
of Europe."

Pierre Beauvais frowned as if he was concen-
trating.

"Do you mean that your uncle is François Dumont?"

"Yes."

"Then of course I have heard his name, although
I have never heard him play."

"Even abroad he was a great success," Zaza said,
"but he wanted to travel, and he wandered round
the world, sometimes giving concerts, sometimes just
meeting people. He wanted to find those who were
interested in music and poetry, the two things to
which he has devoted his life."

"Symbolism does not only mean poetry."

"I know it includes prose," Zaza replied, "and
my uncle has written two books."

"I must read them."

"I am sure they have been out of print for a
long time."

"Then perhaps you will lend them to me?"

"I would, if I had them with me."

"If I cannot read them you must tell me about them so that I can discuss them with your uncle and tell him how clever I think he is."

"You should not say so unless it is what you really think," Zaza retorted almost severely.

"I think he is the most brilliant man I have ever met in my life, to have a niece as beautiful and as charming as you!"

Now he had embarrassed her again and Zaza said hesitatingly:

"I think ... perhaps it is ... incorrect for you to ... speak to me like that"

"Incorrect?" Pierre Beauvais questioned, raising his eye-brows. "It may be unconventional but you are a Symbolist and Symbolists are against everything that is conventional and stereotyped. They believe in expressing what they feel. And I am doing just that."

"I ... think I should ... stop you."

"Do you dislike my speaking the truth?"

"Not exactly dislike ... but it makes me feel ... shy."

"I know that, and I find it is the most fascinating thing that has happened to me for a very long time."

There was a pause before he said, almost as if he spoke to himself:

"I had forgotten that women could blush and look as if the world were an unspoilt, beautiful place with nothing ugly or evil in it."

The way he spoke made Zaza say:

"You sound as if ... something has ... shocked or ... upset you"

"Perhaps you are right," he said, "but I do not want to talk about that, only about you.

Zaza was wondering how she could prevent him from doing so when their omelettes arrived. Because they were so delicious and she was hungry, she ate for a little while without speaking.

"Surely you brought some food with you on the train?" Pierre Beauvais asked. "It is a long journey from Dorné to Paris."

"I am afraid we forgot to take ... anything with

... us, but my uncle bought something to eat at two of the stations."

"I can see that what you need is somebody to look after you."

Pierre Beauvais spoke in a caressing tone which made Zaza feel once again how fortunate she was that he was there.

She did not speak and after a moment he said:

"As I realise you have not been in Paris before, I want to tell you that you must not in any circumstances walk about alone."

She looked at him in dismay.

"But my uncle may not be well enough to accompany me."

"Then you will have to stay in the Hotel with him, unless you will permit me to take his place."

"It is very ... kind of you to ... suggest it," Zaza replied, "but I am sure you have more ... important things you ... wish to do."

"On the contrary, I can think of nothing more important than showing you Paris."

"It would be wonderful!" she said impulsively. "But perhaps it would be ... wrong."

"Wrong?" he questioned in a puzzled voice.

She realised that once again she had forgotten that she was not the Princess Marie-Celeste behaving in an outrageous manner, but merely *Mademoiselle* Dumont, who could quite reasonably, since her uncle was indisposed, accept the companionship of a man of whom he approved.

Because she felt she had made a slip, she said:

"I think it ... wrong to take up so much of your time. But if you would show me a little of Paris, I would find it very ... thrilling."

"There is a great deal of Paris to see," Pierre Beauvais replied, "so I warn you it will take a long time."

Zaza wondered what he would say if she told him that the length of time depended on how long her money lasted.

Then, thinking of money made her realise that

she could not allow him to spend on her the little he possessed.

But she had a feeling that if she said anything to him he would refuse categorically to let her pay for herself.

'I must talk to the Professor,' she thought. 'He must give Pierre Beauvais back the money he has spent on entertaining me.'

"What are you worrying about?" Pierre Beauvais asked.

"How do you . . . know I am . . . worrying?" Zaza parried.

"Your eyes manage to be both expressive and mysterious," he said. "There is something about you I do not understand. At the same time, I feel I can read your thoughts and be aware of many things you are feeling."

"Now you are making me . . . nervous!" Zaza protested. "I do not wish that . . . anybody should read my . . . thoughts."

"Why not?"

"Because they are . . . secret."

"I do not wish you to have secrets from me."

He spoke in such an intimate manner that she felt she must argue with him.

"How can you possibly say that?" she asked. "We have only just met each other, and then in a very . . . unusual manner."

"That is a practical way of stating what happened," Pierre Beauvais said, "but as a Symbolist you must know it is not how long you know a person but what you feel about them that counts."

He paused, waiting for her to reply, and because he expected it she said after a moment:

"I suppose . . . you are right."

"Of course I am right," he said. "I knew the moment I saw you that you were the woman I have been searching for all my life and had begun to feel did not really exist."

Now he was speaking in a low voice that seemed to vibrate through her, and after a moment as she did not reply he went on:

"Perhaps we were together in another existence, in other lives, but I feel that I know you and that your thoughts are my thoughts, your feelings my feelings."

Zaza sipped the wine that had been poured out for her.

She did not know why, but when he spoke to her like that, she felt strange little thrills run through her body and found it difficult to breathe.

"You are so lovely," Pierre Beauvais went on, "so exquisitely, unbelievably lovely. I want to lock you up in a glass case where nobody can touch you except myself, and I cannot help feeling that it is crazy for you to come to Paris of all places."

"I cannot ... understand what you are ... saying."

"I think you do," he said. "And now, because I do not want your uncle to feel you are neglecting him, I am suggesting that we finish our meal and I take you back to him."

Zaza had the impulse to cry out that she had no wish to leave.

She wanted to go on talking to him, sitting in this small, intimate little Café with its checked tablecloths and its bare wood floor.

Instead, she refused the cheese that was offered to her, feeling that she was no longer hungry as she had been before, and merely sipped the bitter coffee which was stronger than anything they drank at the Palace.

"Your uncle will see his friends tonight," Pierre Beauvais said as if he was following his train of thought. "We will have supper with him, and because I think you should go to bed early after such a long journey and being in a collision, I will not suggest taking you anywhere else afterwards. But another night we might go dancing."

"Dancing?"

Zaza's eyes lit up.

She had read of places in Paris where people danced in the open air, but she had thought that as she was coming here with the Professor, it was unlikely that she would have an opportunity to go to them.

"We will dance," Pierre Beauvais said firmly. "I am sure you are as light as the proverbial thistle-down, and perhaps because you are such a fairy-creature and not entirely human, your feet will not even touch the ground."

Zaza laughed.

"How embarrassing it would be, after you have said that, if you find me as heavy as a sack of coals."

"I will tell you the truth after we have danced together."

As he spoke he smiled as if he knew for certain what her dancing would be like.

It struck Zaza suddenly that the sort of dancing they did in Paris would be very different from the way they danced at the Palace.

There had been only two Balls given there since she grew up, and then, because of her rank, she had been forced to dance only with the most distinguished Courtiers and aristocrats in Melhausen, who had all seemed extremely old and were certainly not light on their feet.

What was more, she had no idea how to dance the Polka, which she had read was the fashionable dance amongst the young Parisians.

"I will teach it to you" Pierre Beauvais said quietly.

She started as she realised that he was reading her thoughts.

"I have a feeling," he went on, "that because your uncle is a great musician, your knowledge of music is classical rather than modern, so that is something else I must teach you."

"I am afraid I am very . . . ignorant about those . . . sort of . . . things," Zaza said.

"Yet you are wise about the things that matter," Pierre Beauvais replied.

She was not quite certain what he thought mattered, but she liked the idea of his thinking her wise and therefore she smiled in response.

He finished his glass of wine and called for the bill.

Once again Zaza wondered if he could possibly afford to pay for her, but she made no suggestion that she should pay for her share.

She was sure that if she did, he would instantly dismiss the idea. At the same time, she was aware that she did not know, if he accepted, how much she should offer him.

'I must try to understand French money,' she thought, and knew she would have to get the money she had brought from Melhausen changed.

Their currency was also in francs, but she had the idea, although she was not quite certain, that they were lower in value than the French franc and she would therefore not get as much for a twenty-franc note as it was worth in Melhausen.

When Pierre Beauvais put the tip under the folded bill, the waiter bowed, saying: *"Merci, Monsieur, merci beaucoup!"*

Zaza rose and picked up her handbag and gloves. which had been lying on the vacant chair beside her.

They were bowed out by the Proprietor of the Café.

When they stepped into the street, Pierre Beauvais put his hand under her elbow to help her through the crowds who were moving quickly or staring into the illuminated shop-windows.

As he touched her Zaza felt a thrill run through her and she told herself it was because no man had ever before touched her in such an intimate manner.

'I should feel the same whoever I was with.' she thought to herself, knowing that that was untrue.

It was not far to the Hôtel des Champs and when they stepped inside, the Concierge said to Zaza:

"You are back, *M'mselle!* The Doctor has just arrived and is upstairs with *Monsieur."*

"Thank you," Zaza said. "I will go up to him at once."

She turned to Pierre Beauvais.

"Thank you very much," she said, "for being so kind and giving me such a delicious meal."

"You know without my saying so that it was a very great pleasure," he replied.

Because once again she felt shy, she turned away quickly and hurried up the stairs.

She climbed them so swiftly that she was almost breathless by the time she reached the third floor.

She knocked on the Professor's door, heard his reply, and entered the room.

The Doctor, a middle-aged man with a beard, was standing by the bed.

He looked at her as she appeared and was obviously surprised by what he saw.

"This is my niece," the Professor explained, then said to Zaza: "Let me introduce you, my dear, to *Monsieur* Sachet, who has been most kind and encouraging."

"Your uncle fortunately has not broken any bones in his leg," the Doctor said, "but it is badly sprained and he must rest it and certainly not attempt to walk for the next few days."

"That is very sad for him," Zaza replied. "He was so looking forward to seeing Paris."

"To lie here in Paris itself is almost sufficient," the Professor said, "and it is a great relief to know that even though it is so painful there is nothing seriously wrong."

"You have been fortunate," the Doctor said. "And now that I have seen your niece, I am sure I am leaving you in good hands."

"I will certainly do my best to make my uncle obey your instructions," Zaza said.

The Doctor smiled at her as if he appreciated how pretty she looked.

Then as he turned to shake hands with the Professor, he saw standing on a table by the bedside the little bottle of drops which somebody—Zaza thought it must have been Pierre Beauvais—had taken from the Professor's pocket when he was undressed.

The Doctor dropped his hand before the Professor could grasp it, and as he took up the bottle of drops he asked:

"What are these?"

"They are for my heart," the Professor said quickly.

"So you have heart trouble!"

"Only times. It is nothing but a tiresome tremor which makes me breathless and a little faint."

The Doctor looked at the drops again and pursed his lips together.

"You are making light of what might be serious," he said. "If you have any trouble of that sort, send for me immediately."

He looked at Zaza.

"Do not forget, *Mademoiselle,* hearts can be tricky, and dangerous if they are neglected."

"My uncle was upset after the collision on the train," Zaza said. "But when I gave him the drops he revived immediately."

"Then he should always have them with him," the Doctor said, "and if you are worried, I do not live far away."

"You are very kind," Zaza said. "I shall not forget."

The Doctor held out his hand to the Professor.

"Good-bye, Professor. I remember hearing you play when I was at the Sorbonne. I felt myself transported into a world I did not even know existed. You were an inspiration to me in those days."

"Thank you, thank you!" the Professor said. "It is gratifying to think that I am not completely forgotten."

"Certainly not amongst those of my age," the Doctor replied, "but alas, the young do not appreciate music as we did."

"No, indeed," the Professor said with a sigh.

The Doctor turned to Zaza.

"*Au revoir, Mademoiselle.* Are you also a pianist?"

"Only an amateur one," Zaza answered, "but I like to hear my uncle playing."

"I am sure he finds such a lovely audience some

compensation for the fact that like me he is growing old," the Doctor said. "I shall be waiting to hear from you if you need me, *Mademoiselle*."

"Thank you very much, *Monsieur*," Zaza replied.

She saw the Doctor to the top of the stairs, then went back into the Professor's room.

"I am sorry, so sorry that you have to rest for so long," she said sympathetically.

"I was so afraid of having broken a bone and having to wear splints or plaster," the Professor replied, "that I am only too delighted it is not worse."

"If you are happy, then so am I," Zaza said, "but you heard what the Doctor said. You must allow *Monsieur* Beauvais to have you carried downstairs when it is time to meet your friends."

"As long as I can meet them I do not care how I get there," the Professor said. "Tonight there will be a reunion, and now at last *ma Princesse*, you will meet intelligent men, men with feelings, men with hearts that pulsate for what is right and just and most of all for freedom!"

The Professor's voice rang out in the small room, but Zaza was not listening.

She was thinking once again how fortunate she was that Pierre Beauvais was there and that he would arrange everything, even helping the Professor to dress and getting him downstairs to the Café.

'What would I do without him?' she wondered.

* * *

Looking round the Café des Champs, Zaza thought it was not in the least what she had expected.

She had somehow thought the Café would be a larger edition of the place where Pierre Beauvais had taken her earlier in the evening.

Instead she found that it was in the basement of the Hôtel des Champs and was a large, smoke-filled room with walls decorated with rough sketches which she supposed had been done by Impressionists.

There were no cloths on the bare tables and

she found the other diners very unlike the French types she was expecting.

They were mostly men, although there were a few women wearing strange clothes and with painted faces that appeared to Zaza somewhat vulgar.

At the far end of the room in a corner was a large table with the Professor's friends seated round it, who seemed even stranger in appearance than the diners at the other tables.

Most of them were wearing capes and wide-brimmed black felt hats, and Zaza thought many of them were not as well bred as she had expected.

She had always thought that as the Professor was very cultured and came from a good family, his friends would be the same or perhaps would belong to an even higher stratum of society than he did himself.

But a number of the men who sat round the table and greeted him effusively when they arrived were, she thought, not the refined, intellectual types she had expected. Some of them were a little common and even in some ways rough in their appearance.

However, they greeted her with great politeness and accepted Pierre Beauvais when the Professor introduced him as a friend and benefactor.

He told them about the train collision and was placed at the table in as comfortable a position as possible with his leg resting on a stool.

Pierre Beauvais even arranged for some cushions to be brought which would prop him up in his chair.

Then food and wine were ordered, but Zaza noted that several of the men at the table were content with the wine and did not wish to eat anything.

She, on the other hand, allowed Pierre Beauvais to order the dishes he thought she would enjoy and when they were brought after rather a long wait she found that they were delicious.

He ordered food for the Professor as well, but he was too busy to eat more than a few mouthfuls before he allowed the dish in front of him to grow cold.

At first the Professor talked only of the past, of the letters that had been exchanged and of the way in which they had all remained close friends even while he was in Melhausen and they were in Paris.

Finally, when they had been in the Café for perhaps an hour, one of the men said:

"Things have progressed, Dumont, since you were last with us. We also have changed."

"Changed?" the Professor asked.

"We are not concerned only with poetry, prose, and music. We leave that to those who frequent the Soleil d'Or."

"That is right," another man remarked. "We have grown away from them, which is why we have come here."

Zaza was surprised at what he was saying, since the Professor had spoken so often of the Soleil d'Or, the Café in the Place St. Michel.

He had told her how it had been started by Leon Deschamps, a poet who had founded an Art and Literary Revue called *La Plume*.

As a magazine it had held *soirées* every Saturday, when the contributors would crowd into the Café to perform, reciting their poems or reading their articles to the enthusiastic applause of the other diners.

Zaza had in fact longed to go to the Soleil d'Or and had expected that while they were in Paris the Professor would take her there.

She had been surprised to learn that instead he was to meet his friends at the Café des Champs, but now she understood and only hoped he would not be disappointed.

"You did not mention in the letter I received from you two days ago that you had left the Soleil d'Or for any particular reason," he remarked.

"We left because they were no longer serious enough for us," one of his friends answered.

"In what way?" the Professor asked.

The man to whom he was speaking glanced

over his shoulder as if to see that they were not overheard before he replied:

"We have despaired of obtaining reforms by peaceful means. That is why we have decided to act!"

The Professor raised his eye-brows and enquired:

"What do you mean by that?"

"We mean that only by waging war on the State can we attain any advance."

"We have talked of this so often before," the Professor replied. "We all are aware that it is freedom we seek. We all believe that our minds are stifled by the class which has gained power in France and which is determined to allow nothing new to be accepted by the Bourgeoisie."

There was a cry from round the table.

"The Bourgeoisie! Those are our enemies! It is they who must be assassinated by any means at hand!"

The Professor sat up stiffly in his chair.

"Assassinated?" he questioned.

"We have to be rid of them," one of his friends answered. "We have talked and talked and it has got us nowhere. Now we are advocating propaganda by deed."

The Professor shook his head.

"You are going too fast. At the same time, I understand that you are all feeling frustrated and we must fight harder for our beliefs and our faith."

"Hard indeed!" another man said. "You will find, Professor, that it is the knife that purges and the bomb that cleanses!"

Zaza felt herself shiver.

It was not only what the speaker had said but the way he had said it, and she had the feeling that the Professor, still thinking ecstatically of his ideals, did not fully comprehend that these men round the table were speaking seriously.

She glanced at Pierre Beauvais and saw that he was listening intently, but he said nothing.

She wondered what he felt, then told herself

that it was she who did not understand exactly what was being said, and how could she be expected to when she had never met such people before?

Vaguely at the back of her mind she recalled hearing that there had been a lot of unrest in France and that a young fanatic had thrown vitriol in the Paris Stock Exchange and fired three revolver-shots which had not harmed anyone.

The newpapers in Melhausen had said that he was a lunatic and not to be taken seriously.

Now she remembered that in December last year, a display of revolutionary activity had taken place in the French Parliament.

A number of Deputies were engaged in debate at four o'clock in the afternoon, when a bomb was thrown from one of the public galleries.

It exploded in mid-air with a deadly shower of metal nails.

The newspapers had reported that when the smoke cleared, several Deputies and members of the public were found to be wounded by inch-long nails, but no-one was killed.

In fact, the sitting had resumed twenty minutes later, after the wounded had been treated and order had been restored.

Zaza had read that the bomb-thrower, Auguste Vaillant, had been caught. He was a young man whose life had been one of unbelievable misery and disillusionment.

He admitted that he wanted to strike a blow in the Chamber of Deputies and he blamed the Members of the Government for the social miseries of the country.

Looking back, Zaza remembered that he had said his explosion was "the cry of a class which demanded its rights and which will soon match deeds to words."

She recalled not only the report in the newspapers but also thinking that the fact that the young man had been condemned to death, although he had killed nobody, was unfair.

She had felt it was a miscarriage of justice and had said so to the Professor but not to her father, who had inevitably thought that the sentence was both right and just.

The Professor had agreed that the sentence was too harsh.

The young man had died bravely shouting as he was led to the guillotine: "Death to all Bourgeois society, and long live anarchy!"

He had been a martyr of class war and Zaza could understand that the Professor's friends felt rebellious and wished to change the law, or perhaps the people who administered it.

At the same time, she was certain that they were only talking on a grandiose scale about fighting and bombing and would be far from willing to face the guillotine.

They were very busy with words that would certainly not be translated into deeds outside the Café.

The Professor listened while one man told him things which had obviously been omitted from their letters.

"We are not the only ones," he said, "who believe that something should be done and done quickly!"

"There are many of us?" the Professor enquired.

"You have lived in Melhausen for too long," a friend said. "Now there are a hundred groups like ourselves, all committed to the idea of action."

The Professor looked surprised and the speaker went on:

"The people of Paris are already so scared that many landlords of apartments go to the length of advertising the fact that no lawyers or policemen live on their premises!"

He laughed rather unpleasantly.

"Are you telling me that war is to be declared on everyone connected with the State?" the Professor asked.

"Exactly!" another of his friends replied. "Only by destroying the whole structure of the State as it is today can we build a better one without the Bourgeoisie."

"That is impossible!" the Professor exclaimed.

"Why?"

There was silence for a moment, then the man said:

"Perhaps you have never heard, Professor, what Emile Henry said when he was convicted of hurling a bomb in the Café Terminus near the St. Lazare station."

The Professor knitted his brow as he concentrated.

"Was that when twenty people were wounded?"

"Yes, and Emile Henry claimed that he also made the bomb that killed five men in the Police Station in the Rue des Enfants."

"Tell the Professor what he said before the judges," someone urged, and a man with a soft, low, compelling voice recited:

" 'We wish neither to show mercy nor to stumble, and we shall always march onwards until the revolution; the final aim of our efforts shall have come at last to crown our work by freeing the world.' "

There was silence for a moment, then the man added:

"We have printing-presses turning out papers and broadsheets that tell our readers how to overthrow the social and political system by armed action."

"How are they expected to do that?" the Professor asked a little cynically.

"They have instructions not only on how to fight but how to make bombs at home."

"And if they throw them, there is the guillotine!" the Professor said sharply.

"Only if they are caught!"

"Yes, of course, and I have read, although I did not connect it with you, that the Government is very concerned and determined to stamp out any revolutionary clubs and take stringent action against anyone concerned in what they consider anarchism."

"The Government is beginning to panic," someone said triumphantly. "In fact I am told all the Ministers live in terror of what will happen to them next."

Zaza looked from one to the other of them in perplexity. This was certainly not what she had expected from the Professor's friends and she wondered if he was as bewildered as she was.

Always they had talked together of the beauty and the expressiveness of Symbolistic poetry and of music, which could portray the same ideals and find new horizons for the mind.

But this was the destruction of the body, in fact of innocent people who in most cases, Zaza thought, were doing their own small job to the best of their ability.

There was silence, then the Professor said uncertainly:

"Of course we wish to free the world, we are all agreed on that. But I do not think such methods will be successful."

He himself, Zaza thought, might have thrown a bomb!

A babel of sound burst out, everyone talking at once, their words falling over one another, declaring what had been achieved and accentuating the fact that the Government was already in a state of nervous terror and approaching something like panic.

When he could make himself heard the Professor said:

"I still think that is not the way to achieve our aims, and many who only want to change the thinking of France will be repressed and perhaps imprisoned."

"No, no, you are wrong!" his friends shouted and the noise started all over again.

It lasted for more than an hour and it was Pierre Beauvais who brought the evening to an end.

"I think," he said in a quiet but clear voice when the wordy protagonists had paused for a drink, "that the Professor should go to bed. He has had a very long day, has been injured, and is still in considerable pain. I am sure you can continue this extremely interesting discussion tomorrow."

For a moment everybody looked at him in surprise.

He had not said anything the whole evening and Zaza thought that they must suspect him of being completely inarticulate.

Because she thought he needed support, she said quickly:

"*Monsieur* Beauvais is right. My uncle is very tired. The Doctor said he must rest, and I feel he would be extremely annoyed if he knew where his patient was at this moment."

"You have a very pretty Nurse, Professor!" someone remarked and they all laughed good-humouredly.

Pierre and another man carried the Professor up to his bedroom and when they reached it Zaza saw that he was exhausted but still ready to argue.

"They are wrong, they are quite wrong!" he said to Pierre Beauvais as he and the other man set him down on the bed.

"You can tell them so tomorrow," Pierre replied. "Now you have to go to sleep, and the quicker we get you into bed the better."

He glanced at Zaza as he spoke and she knew he wanted her to leave the room.

She walked to the Professor's side.

"Good-night, Uncle François," she said. "And thank you for a very interesting and exciting evening."

"It was exciting," the Professor murmured.

Zaza smiled at him and went from the room.

In her room on the other side of the passage she began to undress, thinking that never before in her life had she spent such an extraordinary evening nor had she imagined that supper in Paris could be so very different from what she had expected.

Could the Professor's friends really be serious? she wondered.

She could not help thinking that their talk of

throwing bombs and killing the Bourgeoisie was just talk, rather like young soldiers who boast of how if there was a war they will kill thousands of the enemy.

At the same time, there was something about the way the men in the Café had talked which made Zaza shiver.

Now for the first time it struck her that the Symbolists she had come to find were in fact anarchists!

It seemed incredible—completely and absolutely incredible that not only was the Professor involved with such people but so was she.

She had the sudden feeling that if they knew who she was, her life might be in danger.

Every Court in Europe had been afraid when four years ago, in 1890, attempts had been made on the lives of the King of Italy, the German Emperor, the King of Spain, and the Russian Tsar.

She remembered the precautions her father had taken at the time whenever he and her mother went driving about the Capital.

For at least a year the conversation in the Palace at Melhausen had been of the horrors of anarchism and the threat it could present to every Crowned Head.

But then the excitement had died down and the Monarchs of Europe, while still thinking they were in some danger, slept more peacefully in their beds. But now it was the turn of the middle-class.

"Anarchism!" Zaza murmured to herself, and felt herself shiver with a sudden fear.

A knock on the door made her start simply because she had not expected it and her thoughts were frightening her.

"Who is . . . it?" she asked with a little quiver in her voice.

"It is I, Pierre."

Zaza felt her heart leap, but now it was not with fear. She ran to the door.

"What is it?" she asked without opening it.

"I only wanted to tell you that your uncle is

very comfortable and was asleep before we had finished undressing him."

"Thank you . . . thank you very much . . . you are very kind."

There was silence for a moment and she thought perhaps he had gone away. Then he said.

"I shall see you tomorrow. Will you have break-fast with me?"

"Breakfast?"

"Downstairs, not where we were tonight but in the Restaurant which is on the ground floor. Shall I meet you there at eight-thirty? Or would you rather it was later?"

"Eight-thirty would be very . . . convenient," Zaza replied.

"I will be waiting, *Bon soir, Mademoiselle.*"

"*Bon soir, Monsieur,* and thank you . . . thank you very much . . . indeed!"

She listened to his footsteps receding down the uncarpeted passage.

Then as she continued to get ready for bed she was no longer frightened; instead, her heart was sing-ing.

She would see him tomorrow!

Chapter Four

Zaza stood under the shade of a tree feeling that the heat was almost overpowering.

Then as she felt a faint breeze coming from the Seine she turned eagerly towards it, pulling her hat off her head as she did so.

She had not thought the hat in which she had travelled, which was the only one she had brought with her, was really smart enough to go out with Pierre Beauvais, but as he had insisted that she must not go out shopping by herself, there was nothing she could do but put on the same small-brimmed straw hat with its blue ribbons.

She was wearing a thin pink muslin gown, and when they went into the street she stopped at the first flower-seller.

"How remiss of me," Pierre said. "I intended to buy you some flowers and thought I would do so on our way home."

"I only want one," Zaza said with a little smile.

He looked surprised but when she opened her handbag to pay, he insisted on doing so.

She took a rose, a pale pink one just coming into bloom, and by glancing at her reflection in the plain glass of a shop-window she managed to fix the rose exactly where she wanted it on the crown of her hat.

"Perfect!" Pierre Beauvais approved.

Zaza thought it was rather attractive and made her feel as if she really was a part of Paris.

Now she put her hat down on the parapet beside her and felt the breeze on her forehead and in her hair, and thought that she felt too free to be confined by anything, even by the convention of wearing a hat.

Feeling an excitement she dared not put into words, she had run down the stairs after saying good-morning to the Professor, to find Pierre waiting for her in the small Restaurant on the ground floor.

It was here that most of the guests who were staying in the Hotel ate their meals if they were *en pension* and Zaza learnt that it was also open to casual customers who did not like the crowded Café in the basement below.

There were only two other people having breakfast, and Zaza thought with a little blush how intimate it was to be sitting at a table alone with a man and be able to talk to him without being overheard.

She could not help wondering what the Countess Glucksburg would say if she knew.

"Today," Pierre Beauvais said, "I am going to take you to see a little of Paris, and as the weather is so lovely I think it would be a mistake to be anywhere but outdoors."

"Yes, of course," Zaza agreed, "and I want to see the Paris of Baron Haussmann, which I have read is now the most beautiful City in Europe."

"I think so," Pierre Beauvais said, "but then I am a Frenchman."

"I too am French," Zaza said.

He looked at her a little quizzically, and because she thought he was suspicious she said quickly:

"There are other nationalities in my make-up, but today I want to think myself entirely a part of *la Belle France.*"

"And a very beautiful part!" Pierre Beauvais said quietly.

Zaza realised that once again he was making her feel embarrassed.

However, it was impossible to feel anything but excitement as they walked along the Rue de Rivoli beside the Tuileries Gardens and finally, after eulogising over the Place de la Concorde, found themselves alongside the Seine.

"I want to stop," Zaza said. "I want to look at the river of which I have heard so much."

Now she saw that it was a sheet of gold in the sunshine and wider and more majestic than she had expected and of course even more entrancing.

The fine buildings on either side, the bridges spanning the river, the barges with their cargo moving slowly over the flowing water—all was an enchantment.

"It is lovely ... lovely!" she exclaimed.

"That is what I think," Pierre Beauvais said, but he was looking at her face and not at the river.

There was a silence for a little while, then he said.

"Tell me what you thought about the supper-party last night."

Zaza had been expecting him to ask her this before now.

She did not reply for a moment and her eyes were troubled.

"It was so ... different from what I had ... expected," she said at length.

"What did you expect?"

"That his friends would be exactly like the Prof ... I mean ... my uncle," she replied. "Idealistic, carried away by art into a kind of ... dream-world they have ... invented for themselves."

"A very good description," Pierre Beauvais said.

"But then ... last night ..." Zaza began, then stopped.

"I want you to tell me what you thought about it," he insisted.

"They could not be ... serious ... could they?" Zaza asked.

"That is what I was wondering myself."

"I thought they were just being dramatic, threatrical! The way they wrote to Uncle François was very . . . different."

"What did they say in their letters?"

"They spoke of course of Symbolism, and of how much they wanted to be free of the Bourgeoisie, but they never even hinted that they . . . wished to . . . take a . . . violent course."

Zaza paused for a moment and she knew that Pierre Beauvais was listening to her intently.

After a second or two she went on:

"My uncle showed me the letters he received and they all called for the return of mystery, dreams, and symbols to the art of poetry."

"That is the true spirit of Symbolism," Pierre Beauvais said.

"I always . . . understood," Zaza went on hesitantly, "that its whole . . . object was not to convey . . . precise understanding . . . but to suggest and . . . evoke feelings as . . . music does."

"You are right," Pierre Beauvais said. "It is the suggestion and the symbol which counts, not the object itself."

"Feeling like that," Zaza argued, "how can they change so quickly as to want only . . . violence?"

She made a little gesture with her hands as she said:

"Can you imagine my uncle trying to kill anyone, least of all somebody he does not even know?"

Pierre Beauvais did not speak and after a moment she said:

"You do not . . . think they are . . . serious?"

"I have not yet made up my mind," Pierre said. "Like you, I was shocked and surprised by what I heard last night, but of course it may be just playacting with words."

"I am sure it is . . . it must be!"

Zaza gave a little sigh.

"I am so . . . disappointed."

"Why?"

"Because I expected to hear music, to listen to poetry being recited by its author, and to feel myself carried away by the modern poets of France."

Pierre Beauvais smiled, then he said very softly:

"When with sunlight in your hair, in the street
And in the evening, you appeared to me laughing
And I thought I saw the fairy with the hat of
                                                brightness."

Zaza gave a little cry of delight and clapped her hands.

"Mallarmé!"

"You are right."

"That is exactly what I wanted to hear, although I admit that at times I find him difficult to understand. I have read many of his works, nearly all of them, I think, but however hard I think and think about . . . some of them, I cannot . . . translate to myself exactly what he is trying to say."

"I think," Pierre Beauvais replied, "the drama which is central to his work is that of the death of being and the resurrection of consciousness."

There was silence for a moment while Zaza thought about what he had said.

She looked puzzled and was too honest to pretend that she understood, and Pierre said with a hint of laughter in his voice:

"Forget Mallarmé and let me recite to you a poem which you can understand quite easily."

She raised her eyes and he said in his deep voice:

"God made the world
       Everything in its place.
   The sun, the moon, the rainbow,
       And your perfect face."

For a moment Zaza looked surprised, then she asked:

"Did . . . you write that?"

"I wrote it last night to you."

She blushed and felt shy but she tried to say in quite an ordinary tone:

"That was . . . clever of you because it is . . . good."

"It is true."

"I am . . . flattered that you should have . . . written a poem to me. No-one has ever . . . done that . . . before."

"I can only imagine that you live walled up in a tower, or else despite your uncle's talents you have not met many poets."

Poets certainly did not abound in the Palace, Zaza thought.

The idea of any of the men in attendance upon her father writing a poem was so amusing that she was smiling without realising it, and Pierre Beauvais asked:

"What is amusing you? Not, I hope, my humble efforts to express my consciousness?"

"No, of course not," Zaza said quickly. "I was just thinking how different my life is . . . here from the . . . one I have been . . . living in Melhausen."

"Then you do not always live with your uncle?" Pierre Beauvais asked perceptively.

"No, with my other . . . relations."

"I imagine they are very different from the Professor."

"Very, very different," she said. "They do not understand poetry or music or that it is important to . . . think."

"So you have had to do those things for yourself?"

"With the help of my uncle."

"Now I am beginning to understand some of the things that puzzled me," Pierre Beauvais said.

Because she was afraid he would go on talking about her home, Zaza did not like to ask what those things were. Instead she said:

"I have tried to write poetry, but I find it easier

to express what I am feeling when I am playing the piano."

"I would like to hear you play."

"You must listen to my uncle. He is a real musician."

"I want to listen to what you are saying with your fingers," Pierre Beauvais said.

Zaza thought that might be too revealing and she merely looked away from him and stared at the river, thinking it was so lovely that the picture of it must remain always in her mind.

When she was back in the Palace and feeling lonely and unhappy it would be something she could recall and it would give her the same feeling that she had now.

"You are looking sad," Pierre Beauvais said. "What is worrying you?"

"It is ... nothing I can ... talk about," Zaza said quickly.

"Why not?" he enquired. "I thought as we were getting to know each other so well, we could discuss everything together, even what you are feeling when your eyes look sad and your lips droop a little."

There was something caressing and sympathetic in the way he spoke which made Zaza long to tell him everything.

She felt he would understand if she told him how she had escaped, if only for a very short while, from the confines of her "painted prison."

She wanted to tell him that she was afraid of the future when she would be forced to marry a Prince she had never seen and leave Melhausen for another Palace, undoubtedly exactly the same and from which there would be no escape.

Then she thought that if she told him the truth he might consider it his duty to rebuke the Professor for bringing her away in the first place.

He might look like a poet, he might be a Symbolist, but his behaviour so far as she was concerned struck her as being almost as correct and strict as that of her father or the Countess Glucksburg.

He had forbidden her to walk about the streets unaccompanied and he had been most careful not to embarrass her in any way by undressing the Professor when she was present.

He had, it was true, taken her out alone to dinner and even suggested he might take her dancing.

But she had the feeling that the halls where they would dance would not be the wildly improper ones which she believed existed in Montemartre, but the more conventional places she had read about which were situated near the Champs Élysées.

She might be wrong about him. At the same time, she dared not take a chance by confiding her secrets unless she was sure what his reaction would be.

Pierre Beauvais's voice broke in on her thoughts.

"You are so lovely with the sunlight on your hair," he said. "I feel a dozen poems forming themselves in my mind, and yet where you are concerned I think the poet who could really do you justice has yet to be born."

"If I listen to you I shall become very conceited," Zaza said with a smile. "I think actually it is the magic of Paris which is inspiring you and not my humble self."

"That is untrue and you know it," Pierre Beauvais said, "but I want to know so much about you before I compose any further. Have you ever been kissed?"

His question took her by surprise and Zaza started and was about to reply when she found that his face was very close to hers.

She was suddenly overwhelmingly conscious of him as a man.

With difficulty she found her voice and said:

"I . . . I think, *Monsieur*, you have . . . no right to ask me a . . . question like . . . that!"

"I know the answer without your having to give it to me," he replied, "and that is why I want, as I have never wanted anything in my whole life before, to be the first."

Zaza was about to reply indignantly that she

would not allow anyone, whoever he might be, to
kiss her. Then as she opened her lips to speak, her
eyes met Pierre Beauvais's and somehow it was impossible to move.

She did not know how it happened, but suddenly there was nothing in the whole world but the
sunshine and him.

Everything else seemed to fade away, to move
in an incredible manner out of her mind and out
of her life, so that her father, the Palace, her life as
a Princess, everything, slipped away into oblivion.

There was just the expression in Pierre's eyes
and the feeling, although he had not moved, that
she was close against him and she could not escape.

She wanted to speak, she wanted to run away
and she wanted to stay, but she could feel her heart
beating in her breast and she felt as if she could
no longer breathe and the whole world was still.

Then as if it was part of poetry and music, as
if it was as natural as the movement of the water
beneath them and the air they breathed, his arms
went round her and his lips found hers.

For a moment Zaza was not even sure what she
felt or if what was happening was not merely a part
of her imagination.

But the beating of her heart became a wave
that swept warm and wonderful through her body to
reach her breasts and her throat until it became part
of her lips and Pierre's lips, and they were no longer
two people but one.

She could not explain it even to herself, but it
was a rapture and a glory that was like the sunshine.

She felt as if it was the melody which was in
the air and in her heart, and was not only physical
but a glory that she knew existed somewhere outside
herself and yet was part of her mind and her imagination.

It was so perfect, so wonderful, so rapturous that
she thought she must have died and this was Heaven.

And yet she knew that she was very much alive,
and living and breathing as the leaves fluttering in

the tree above them were alive, and like Paris itself.

She felt Pierre's lips become more insistent, more demanding. Something within her leapt to answer what he asked and she became closer to him not only with her body but with her mind.

This was love.

This was what she had sought with a man. This was why she had known she could not marry without love, for love was life itself.

Pierre raised his head, and because she could not bear the rapture he had given her to end, Zaza gave an inarticulate little murmur of protest.

But because it was impossible to realise what had happened, or to understand the feelings which pulsated through her, she hid her face against his shoulder.

"My darling! My sweet!" he said. "I lay awake all last night thinking of you and knowing, as I did so, that I would feel as I do now."

He felt her quiver and said:

"How can I tell you what I feel except as a poet?"

He was still for a moment as if he was thinking, then he said in a voice that told her how moved he was emotionally:

> *The swirling, floating, pearl-grey mist,*
> *The dawn that wakes the world anew,*
> *The softness of the lips I kissed*
> *The rainbow and the dew,*
> *All I have sought for years to find*
> *Are here in the heart of you.*

Zaza drew in her breath. It was not only what Pierre said, it was the deep note in his voice which moved her and made her vibrate as if to the music of the angels.

Pierre's eyes were on her face.

"That is true," he said, "so true, but I know how inadequate it is to tell you how perfect you are, how beautiful in every way."

He put his fingers under her chin as he spoke and turned her face up to his.

"I am wrong," he said as he looked down at her, "beauty is not in your heart—you are beauty itself. Oh, my darling, how could I know the world held anyone like you and not be aware of it until now?"

Then he was kissing her again, passionately, fiercely, and she felt something like a fire awaken within her and flicker through her body to her lips to meet the fire in his.

He kissed her until she felt as if they left the world behind them, and now there was only themselves high in the sky, enveloped in the light and glory of the sun.

"I love you!" Pierre said.

But Zaza felt as if his voice came from a very long distance away and she could barely hear it.

Then, unexpectedly, so suddenly that she felt as if she might fall to the ground because he was no longer supporting her, he took his arms from her.

"You go to my head, Zaza," he said in a voice which was suddenly different from the way he had been speaking.

Now he leant on the parapet and stared away from her across the river.

Zaza put out her hands in an effort to support herself.

Because he had brought her down so quickly from the heights, for a moment it was impossible to think straight.

She only knew she wanted to be close to him again and she felt lonely and afraid because he was detached and looking away from her.

"What . . . is the . . . matter? What is . . . wrong?" she asked.

"Nothing is wrong."

"You were . . . disappointed when you . . . kissed me?"

He turned round to look at her and she thought there was an expression of pain in his eyes.

"Disappointed?" he repeated. "How could you

imagine such a thing? I have never, and this is true, Zaza, never known a kiss could be so wonderful, so ecstatic, so different in every way from any I have given or received before."

She gave a little sigh of relief. Then she said:

"I was ... afraid when you ... left me."

"I was thinking of you," he said. "When I wanted to kiss you I was thinking of myself and my overwhelming need for you. Then I remembered how young and inexperienced you are and I was afraid that I might spoil anything so perfect."

Zaza was frightened for a moment. Then she asked:

"Do you mean by ... that that you ... think because you kissed me I have become fast, even perhaps ... promiscuous?"

She found it difficult to say the word, and before it had even left her lips Pierre's arms were round her again and he held her close against him.

"Of course not! How could you be anything but pure and perfect, the angel I have been seeking all my life but never thought to find? No, it is not that which worries me, it is just that I have nothing to offer you, my precious, except my love."

"I want ... nothing else," Zaza said quickly.

"Not at the moment, perhaps," Pierre replied, "because now we are living in the present. But unfortunately there is always tomorrow and the future."

"Do not let us think of ... tomorrow," Zaza said quickly. "I only want to live for today. Please ... let us leave the future to take care of itself."

She spoke with passionate intensity, knowing that she had no wish to think of the future. Yet she knew that like the sword of Damocles it always hung over her head; the future when she would have to return to Melhausen to face her father and Prince Aristide.

She felt as if her words gave solace to Pierre.

He pulled her closer against him, and because she had been pleading with him she had looked up and her lips were very close to his.

"We have today, my darling," he said, "and as far as I am concerned it is all I ask of fate and the gods. Today is mine."

He was kissing her again, kissing her in the same demanding way that he had done before and yet Zaza thought there was something different in his kiss.

It was as if he had a sense of urgency so that, like her, he wanted to grasp at the wings of ecstasy, knowing that it could not last forever and that however much they might pretend, tomorrow would come and the day after, and the day after that.

* * *

A long time later Zaza found herself sitting on a chair on the pavement outside a small Café in a side-street where there was very little traffic.

Pierre had ordered their luncheon and while a red-and-white-striped awning protected them from the sun, there was a little breeze that fluttered through the trees which bordered the street on either side.

He ordered the dishes that were, he told Zaza, his favourites and which were cooked at this particular Restaurant better than anywhere else in Paris.

He had also chosen the golden wine that she felt was like drinking sunshine, or perhaps it was because Pierre's eyes were looking into hers and the very air seemed to glitter round them, and once again it was impossible to think of anything but him.

"Perhaps I should have gone...back to see if my uncle is...all right," Zaza said with a little burst of conscience.

"He is not expecting you to," Pierre said. "I saw him before we left while you were putting on your hat and told him I would take you to luncheon somewhere."

"He did not mind?" Zaza asked quickly.

"I think he was almost relieved," Pierre replied.

"He told me he was working out in his thoughts what he should say to his friends tonight and it required his full concentration."

"What can he say, except to urge them to be more sensible? I only hope he is not too disappointed that they are not as he expected them to be."

"I think some of the others are disappointed too," Pierre said consolingly. "There were three men there last night who were about the same age as your uncle and who I was sure disapproved of what those two men Laurent and Boisseau were saying."

"Yes, they were the worst," Zaza said, "and they seemed, in a way it is difficult to describe, to be rather rough. I could not think of them as being poets."

"I should be interested to see their poetry," Pierre said as if he spoke to himself.

"I think Uncle François should insist on everybody reciting aloud as they do in the Café du Soleil d'Or," Zaza said, "then we would know if they are really Symbolists, or . . ."

She stopped and Pierre asked:

"What do you think they were? I would be interested to hear."

"It seems so . . . disloyal somehow, but when they quoted the man who had been . . . guillotined nearly a month ago, I felt they might be . . . anarchists."

Zaza could hardly whisper the word because the idea of anarchy frightened her so terribly.

She thought she would always remember her father when he read of the attempt on the life of the King of Italy, saying:

"These devils will kill us all! Make no mistake—sooner or later we shall be assassinated like Alexander III!"

"It was not anarchists who killed Tsar Alexander," the Grand-Duchess had said quietly.

Zaza had been proud that her mother's voice was not hysterical like her father's.

"I know it was the Nihilists," the Grand-Duke had snapped, "but if you are killed by a bomb it does not really matter what the man who throws it calls himself."

This was indisputably true, and Zaza had been well aware that her father was frightened.

It somehow seemed degrading that a man so full of his own pomp and circumstance, so large and overpowering physically and mentally, should be afraid of dying.

And yet there was no doubt that he was, and she had heard him giving stringent instructions every time they left the Palace so that every possible precaution in securing their safety should be taken.

Only her mother had been calm, and if she had been afraid she never showed it outwardly.

"Are you frightened, Mama?" Zaza had asked her once when there had been reports of another unsuccessful anarchistic attempt on a Crowned Head.

"I am beginning to think I am a fatalist," the Grand-Duchess replied. "If God means us to die, we shall die, and I only hope I shall do so with dignity."

Zaza looked at her mother admiringly.

"I am sure you will, Mama."

The Grand-Duchess had indeed died with dignity, although not by an assassin's hand but painfully and slowly from cancer.

Now Zaza, because she was curious, asked Pierre:

"Are people in Paris as frightened as those men last night were saying they are?"

"There is a certain amount of panic," Pierre replied, "and I think one might describe the Police and the Government as becoming increasingly agitated."

"Have there been many bombs since Emile Henry was guillotined for throwing one?"

"There were two explosions in March," Pierre replied, "and an anarchist blew himself up while attempting to take a bomb into the Church of the Madeleine."

"One almost feels inclined to say it served him right!" Zaza exclaimed. "How dare he take a bomb into a Church! You can hardly call that striking a blow at the Bourgeoisie."

"I think all bomb-throwers are a little mad," Pierre answered, "and of course there have been bogus plots which have caused a lot of people to look extremely stupid because they were taken in by someone playing a hoax on them."

"Tell me about them," Zaza begged.

"There was a bogus plot to blow up the Opera House, and another to blow up the President's Box at the Longchamps race-course."

Zaza was about to ask more questions, but Pierre said:

"If we go on talking about bombs you will begin to frighten yourself into thinking you may be blown up too. But as you are neither Royal nor Bourgeois, I can promise, my sweet, that you are safe."

Zaza wondered what he would say if she revealed that on that count she was very unsafe, but she merely smiled and he went on:

"Also, no man in his senses would want to injure anything so beautiful as you. Let me assure you, my darling, that if it is necessary I will protect you with my life."

They finished their luncheon and now Pierre rested his arms on the table with his face in his hands.

"I want to look at you and go on looking at you," he said. "I adore the way you smile. I find the way your eyes flicker a little when you are shy and the colour rises in your cheeks so entrancing, so breathtakingly lovely, that every time it happens I fall more and more in love with you than I am already!"

Zaza made a helpless little gesture.

"How can this . . . happen? How can we . . . feel like this so . . . quickly?"

"There is no time where lovers are concerned," Pierre answered. "Love comes in a flash, like lightning or an arrow from Cupid's bow winging its way through the air into one's heart."

He smiled before he added:

"That is what happened to me yesterday when I saw your face looking out the window of the train. It was the embodiment of all my ideals and everything that had ever meant beauty and poetry to me."

"What were you doing there?" Zaza said. "I never thought to ask you."

"It is quite simple," he replied. "I was in the other train, the one that ran into yours. Now I think it was a rather dramatic means contrived by Cupid to bring us together."

"A very expensive way for the railway!" Zaza laughed.

"But very wonderful for us," Pierre replied.

He did not speak any more, but went on looking at her until Zaza put up her hands like a barrier between them.

"You are not to look any more," she said, "otherwise you will find a dozen flaws! Then you will be disappointed, and I shall feel I must go away and never see you again."

"If that happened," Pierre said, "what do you think I would feel at losing you?"

There was a note in his voice which Zaza did not understand and after a moment she said:

"I like being here . . . and I like talking to you . . . but I think we ought to go . . . back."

"Why?"

"I am thinking of my uncle."

"I am sure he will be perfectly happy without you, and I do not think for one second he needs you as I do."

As he spoke Pierre moved to put his hands down on the table and hold them out towards Zaza.

"I need you! I want you!" he said. "Do you not feel in your innermost heart that we were meant for each other?"

She hesitated a moment, then she put both her hands into his and felt his fingers close tightly.

"Answer me!" he commanded.

"I love . . . you!" Zaza said, "although I still cannot . . . believe it has . . . happened."

"And do you belong to me as I think you do?"

Just for a moment Zaza had a quick memory of her father and her position as the Princess Marie-Celeste.

Then she was not aware of anything but the thrills that were running through her because she was touching Pierre, because his eyes were on her lips and she felt as if he kissed her.

He was waiting and after a moment she said in a voice that was barely above a whisper:

"I . . . belong to . . . you."

She saw the fire flare into his eyes and his whole face seemed to be illuminated as if with a divine light.

"Oh, my darling, my sweet!" he said. "That is what I wanted you to say. I know you are mine and have belonged to me since the beginning of time in a dozen different lives, perhaps more, but I wanted you to be sure of it too."

"I . . . am sure," Zaza said, "but it will not be . . . easy."

She was not quite certain what she meant by that, not really knowing what he asked of her. She was only aware that always at the back of her mind was the insurmountable barrier that lay between them; the barrier of rank, the barrier of blood.

She was Royal, she had been brought up to know that she was different from ordinary people, that she had different obligations, different duties.

It was hard to put it into words, but Zaza knew that one of the differences between her and other girls of the same age in Melhausen was that she must marry the man who was chosen for her because it was for the good of the country, not because she was in love with him.

There would in fact be no love in her life unless she became fortunate enough to fall in love with her husband after they were married and he with her.

She knew the odds against that occurring were very great.

Her father and mother had been happy together.

When Zaza was old enough to think of them as people rather than just parents, she was aware that her father was in love with her mother and found her extremely attractive as a woman.

Where her mother was concerned Zaza was not so certain. Certainly she was always charming and outwardly very affectionate to her husband when they were *en famille*.

Yet sometimes Zaza thought there was a wistful expression in her mother's eyes and she seemed to be far away, as if she had withdrawn into a secret world of her own where no-one else could encroach.

But it was not really until after her mother was dead that she wondered if her mother had ever really been wildly, passionately in love with a man and, if so, if it had been with her father.

There was no answer to that question and she had no chance of ever questioning her mother about love.

She had known, as she read many of the poets whom she discussed with the Professor and the books he advised her to ask for from the Palace Library, that what she wanted was the love that she found expressed in a thousand different ways.

It was the love she heard in the music the Professor played on the piano or with his violin, the love she herself felt when she craved for freedom!

It was love which made her feel she must escape from the Palace that encompassed her to the point where she felt suffocated by it.

She knew now, looking at Pierre across the table, that he was what she wanted, he was what she had sensed was waiting for her somewhere in the world if only she could find him.

What he made her feel was love, so majestic, so beautiful, so vividly and compellingly alive that it swept through her body like a tornado and she felt as if she had wings and she was free of everything except her own heart.

Now Pierre, tightening his hold on her fingers, said:

"You have gone away from me and I am afraid I shall lose you. Come back, Zaza! Come back to me!"

She gave a little laugh.

"I am here."

"I want all of you," he answered, "not only your adorable, exquisite body, but your mind, which tries to escape as it did just now."

"How ... do you ... know?" she asked a little incoherently.

"Have you forgotten you are mine and I know everything about you?"

"Everything?" she questioned.

"Everything that is important," he said. "I can look into your soul and see it is perfect, and into your heart, which beats a little faster because we are close again. Zaza, Zaza, how could we possibly contemplate life without each other?"

"I want ... to be with you," Zaza whispered.

She thought even as she spoke that it would be impossible, and she held on to him as if he were a lifeline which must sustain her in a tempestous sea.

*　　*　　*

As they walked back slowly, Pierre taking her through strange little alley-ways and narrow streets which made them reach the Hôtel des Champs very quickly, Zaza told herself that she had never been so happy.

It was as if happiness radiated from her, and Pierre must have noticed it for after a moment he said:

"They say every woman who is in love grows more beautiful than she was before. I have a feeling that by tomorrow I shall have to call in the Military to protect you."

Zaza laughed, then she said:

"They might protect me from ... you!"

"That is what I would be afraid of," Pierre said,

"but strangely, I think your uncle is the only person who would notice no difference in us."

"Uncle François has quite enough to do in thinking about his friends. I feel he will be troubled by what they said last night. Could you reassure him?"

Pierre shrugged his shoulders.

"It is very difficult to know what I can say. I think that Laurent and Boisseau are characters the Symbolist world can do without, but if I criticise them they will undoubtedly expel me from *La Révolte des Coeurs*."

"Then please say nothing!" Zaza said quickly. "If they sent you away it might be more difficult for us to see each other, and I could not bear that to happen."

"Nor could I," Pierre replied.

He thought for a moment, then he added:

"I think we would be wise to sit quietly and just listen to what is going on."

"I am sure Uncle François can influence them not to do anything stupid," Zaza said.

"I think he was very important to the Symbolists in the past," Pierre said, "but he has been away for a long time. I am only sorry that *les Coeurs* moved from the Café du Soleil d'Or."

"So am I," Zaza agreed. "I did so want to go there. I am sure that it is far more amusing than the Café des Champs."

"I will tell you what I will do," Pierre said. "I will suggest to your uncle that you would like to hear some recitations of poetry and some music tonight. I feel sure he will be only too willing to play his violin to at least some of his friends who must have talents other than being able to manufacture home-made bombs."

Zaza gave a little cry.

"No . . . please . . . please do not say such . . . things."

"I am sorry," Pierre Beauvais said instantly, putting his arm round her. "I was only speaking jokingly. As I have already said, no-one would throw a bomb at you, my lovely darling. But if they did, I swear I would protect you."

He was almost laughing at her fears and Zaza knew he did not understand how real they were.

She was intelligent enough to suppose that because she had been four years younger when there had been so many attempts on Monarchs of Europe, it had left a scar upon her consciousness.

She had almost forgotten it, but now it had been revived by the anarchists and their conversation last night.

It all came back: her father's fears, the tension in the Palace, the way she and Rachel had always looked at the crowds when they went driving, wondering if there was someone in them who would kill them simply because they were Royal.

It seemed extraordinary that for the last three years at any rate she had never given a thought to her own safety or imagined that anyone was interested in destroying her simply because she was a Royal Princess.

Now she felt a little tremor of real fear run through her.

"My poor precious, they really have upset you with their ridiculous talk. I shall have to speak to your uncle and tell him that if he cannot control his friends, I shall take you out to dinner so that you will not have to listen to such nonsense."

"Is it . . . nonsense?" Zaza asked.

"I am sure it is!" Pierre Beauvais said consolingly. "Anarchy has become fashionable just as in the last few years we have had Parnassians, Symbolists, Kabbalists, Instrumentalists, and a dozen other movements which have gained temporary fame, only to fade into obscurity when the next excitement came along."

Zaza gave a little cry.

"I am being . . . stupid and you are being very . . . sensible."

"Shall we say you are being feminine?" Pierre said. "And that is what I like. I am terrified of these strident new women who seem to be as fearless as men and much more aggressive."

"I will . . . never be . . . that," Zaza said quickly.

"I will not allow you to be anything but what you are now," he said, "my dream, my ideal, and mine!"

He spoke softly, for they had reached the Hôtel des Champs.

For a moment they stood on the doorstep, looking at each other, and Zaza felt as if Pierre's lips were on hers and he kissed her.

Then with an effort, because she could not bear to think their time together had come to an end, she opened the heavy glass door and walked into the vestibule.

Chapter Five

"Beauvais has told me that you would like to hear poems and music this evening," the Professor said, "and I have told him to try and arrange it."

"Thank you!" Zara exclaimed. "It was what I expected to hear at the Café du Soleil d'Or and what you described to me so often."

"They were amusing, those evenings," the Professor said reminiscently, "but now things are not the same."

He spoke with a note of regret in his voice and Zaza felt that like her he was shocked; shocked by the manner in which his friends had talked last night.

The shock, she thought, doubtless had not been assuaged today when she learnt on her return to the Hotel that he had been visited by several of them in the morning and early afternoon.

"You were not lonely?" she had asked when she went into his bedroom.

She had in fact felt very guilty because she and Pierre had been away for far longer than they had intended.

He had said that love had no time and Zaza had been horrified when she had found that they had left the Professor for so many hours.

It was a relief when he replied:

"No, no! I had visitors in the morning and visitors after luncheon—in fact I found them somewhat tiring and was glad when they went."

From the manner in which he spoke, Zaza was certain that the friends who had tired him had been Laurent and Boisseau, but she was too tactful to say so.

Instead she replied:

"I am glad you were not alone. We walked so far and there was so much to see that I was expecting you to reproach me when I came back."

"I want you to enjoy yourself," the Professor said simply.

Zaza wondered if anyone else would have been so generous.

She talked to the Professor for some time, and when there was a knock on the door, to her surprise it was Dr. Sachet who stood there.

"I was passing, so I came to see how my distinguished patient was keeping," he explained.

"I think he is better," Zaza replied.

Dr. Sachet examined the Professor's ankle and seemed pleased with it.

"If you do not attempt to walk too soon," he said, "it will heal quickly."

"He has been carried every time he has left his bed," Zaza said, and the Doctor's eyes twinkled as he replied:

"I was quite certain the Professor would not lie in bed up here when he might be downstairs in the Café des Champs."

"Come and join us this evening," the Professor invited.

Dr. Sachet shook his head.

"I am too old," he said. "I find that the enthusiastic spoutings of those who wish to change the world over-quickly is exhausting."

"We try to heal the mind as you heal the body," the Professor retorted.

The Doctor laughed.

"Every man to his own task, and I will keep to mine."

He said good-bye to the Professor but when he left the room Zaza followed him.

"I want to ask you something," she said.

The Doctor waited, a look of admiration in his eyes when they rested on her face.

He was thinking that he had never seen a lovelier girl and that the Professor was very fortunate to have such an exquisite niece.

"I have a sister," Zaza said, "who has not been in good health for some time. I was wondering while I was in Paris if I could find anything to help her."

"What is wrong with her?" the Doctor enquired.

Zaza told him how Rachel had grown weaker and more frail month by month, that her back hurt her and, although the Doctors could find nothing wrong with her, the only treatment they could suggest in Melhausen was that she stay almost indefinitely in bed.

"That is wrong," Dr. Sachet murmured, "quite wrong! You are sure that they discovered nothing physically amiss when she was examined?"

"They say there is nothing," Zaza replied. "I am quite certain that if there was, they would have operated on my sister a long time ago."

Dr. Sachet nodded again as if he thought that was very likely. Then he said:

"It is difficult for me to prescribe when I have not seen the patient, but your sister's condition sounds to me very much like a lack of iron and wrong feeding. What does she eat?"

"She is never hungry," Zaza replied. "The Doctors thought she should have a light diet, what my father calls 'slops.'"

"That is just what I expected," Dr. Sachet replied, "and I am going to prescribe something very different. You are to tell your sister she is to eat liver every day, and as much of it as she can consume."

"Liver!" Zaza exclaimed.

"You will find there are various ways of serving it," the Doctor explained, "and you can vary the menu occasionally with kidneys, which are a particular favourite of mine."

He went on to describe a soup which he wanted

Rachel to have, which had to be made with special ingredients which he wrote down.

"This is what Her Majesty the Empress of Austria always takes before she goes hunting," he said. "She is very persnickety about food because she is afraid of getting fat, but this special soup sustains her and gives her strength to ride all day without getting tired."

"I am sure it will help my sister," Zaza said gratefully.

When she looked at what the Doctor had listed she was astonished.

The juices from the best sirloin of beef, from hares, venison, and game in season like partridges and pheasants. Their whole essence was to be condensed into a soup of which the Doctor said one spoonful was as effective as eating several steaks.

."I am sure that will do Rachel good," Zara murmured.

"And one thing more," the Doctor said. "A colleague of mine has been experimenting and has produced from the bones of young animals a powder that can be consumed by human beings."

"Bones?" Zaza questioned.

"My colleague, who is a Professor and a very distinguished one, has found it exceedingly effective for children whose bone-structure has suffered as a result of malnutrition, and he also gives it to elderly patients who suffer too easily from breaks and fractures."

"It sounds very interesting," Zaza said.

"I will bring you some of the bone-powder tomorrow," Dr. Sachet promised. "Please persuade your sister to take at least one spoonful every day. I am sure it will help her."

Zaza thanked him, and when he had left she thought over what he had suggested and was sure it was sensible.

It was certainly different from anything Rachel had tried so far, and every other diet or treatment prescribed by the Court Physicians had proved completely useless.

Because she felt that perhaps she had found exactly what was wanted, Zaza sat down immediately and wrote a long letter to Rachel.

She knew that it would cause comment if she received a letter from Paris, and also they might suspect it came from her.

She therefore enclosed the letter, in which she explained exactly what the Doctor wanted her to do, in another one. This she signed with the name of a French Governess who had taught them several years previously.

Writing in a disguised hand, Zaza said how much she missed the Palace and how often she thought about her "dear pupils."

She was quite certain that if anyone enquired about a letter Rachel had received, they would not bother to read it if it was from *Mademoiselle* Capucine.

At the same time, they would not suspect that there was another letter hidden in the envelope.

Because she was so eager to tell Rachel to start taking the liver at once, as soon as she had finished the letter Zaza sealed it and ran downstairs to give it to the Concierge to post.

She could not help feeling that while she was doing so she might run into Pierre, but there was no sign of him and she wondered how he was occupying his time.

He might, of course, have friends to visit in Paris, but that seemed unlikely considering that when they arrived he had said he had nowhere to stay. It struck her that while he was continually talking about her, she knew nothing about him.

'He is so handsome, so attractive,' she thought to herself, and felt a little apprehensive in case when he was away from her he might find some other woman as interesting as he had found her.

Then she told herself that their love was so overwhelming, so irresistible, that it was something that could not be treated lightly. It was an emotion that could happen only once in a lifetime.

"I love him," she murmured to herself, "and I know he loves me."

As she walked up the stairs she found herself thrilled again when she thought of Pierre's kisses and the feelings he had evoked in her.

"How could I have imagined, how could I have dreamt I would find anyone so wonderful when I came to Paris with the Professor?" she asked herself.

She knew that in a way it was what she had always imagined Paris would be like, golden with sunshine and love.

At the same time, she might not have met Pierre!

Then, as the Professor was confined to his bed, she would have had nothing to do but sit beside him and listen to the conversation of his strange friends.

"I am lucky, so very lucky," Zaza whispered to herself, and said a little prayer of gratitude because not only the Professor but Pierre had changed her life completely.

*   *   *

Later, sitting in the smoke-filled Café des Champs, Zaza thought that if anyone from Melhausen saw her, they would think their eyes were deceiving them.

The Café was even more crowded than it had been the previous evening, and tonight the table in the corner where the Professor sat with his friends was to have, she was told, a very important guest.

The Professor had been excited when he was told that Emile Pouget had invited himself because he had heard that one of the great Symbolists of the past had come to Paris.

"Can he really mean me?" the Professor enquired.

"Of course! And Pouget is only saying what we believe ourselves."

The Professor had been delighted, and Zaza could not help thinking with a little smile that like herself, he had been starved of compliments in Melhausen.

He was only too willing to tell her about Emile Pouget.

"He is editor of *Le Père Peinard*, the most famous and the best-written of all the newspapers which attack the Bourgeoisie."

"I would like to read the newspaper," Zaza remarked.

"I have not seen many copies," the Professor replied, "but those I have read are quite different from the other newspapers, which usually show no talent of any sort."

"Why is *Le Père Peinard* different?" Zaza enquired.

"When I get you a copy," the Professor answered, "you will find it is written entirely in the racing, colourful slang of the Parisian working-class."

"Is that the only difference?"

"No. Pouget has an outstanding talent for writing. His style is not mine, but he is both jovial and grim, hysterical and witty, ribald and deadly earnest."

Zaza laughed.

"It sounds a crazy mixture."

"That is exactly what it is," the Professor agreed. "And because of its impassioned, flowing style, and the quality of its cartoons which are often drawn by gifted and well-known caricaturists, *Le Père Peinard* has a very large circulation."

"How large?" Zaza asked.

"It sells about fifteen thousand copies a week."

"That is a lot!"

"Mind you," the Professor said seriously, "I do not approve of Pouget's ideas, but I have to admire his enterprise."

"I am looking forward to meeting him," Zaza said with a smile.

"I have not met him myself," the Professor admitted, "but I believe he is an embittered ex-clerk who was forced out of his job after he tried to organise a union amongst his fellow-employees."

Zaza began to grow worried.

She had the feeling that the Professor was keeping something from her while trying to make Emile Pouget sound better than he really was.

She was almost certain that he was an anarchist. Then she told herself that she was allowing her impressions of last night to blind her judgment, and she wished she could talk to Pierre and find out what he thought.

She did not, however, have a chance of any private conversation with him when he came up-stairs with a porter to carry the Professor down to the Café.

When she saw him and her eyes met his, she forgot everything except her gladness that he was there.

The thrill that ran through her because he was looking at her in a manner which made her heart stop beating made her long almost uncontrollably to run towards him and feel again the security of his arms.

Instead she forced herself to say in a demure little voice:

"*Bonsoir, Monsieur.*"

"*Bonsoir, Mademoiselle,*" he replied in a tone that said much more than the words.

Most of the Professor's friends were already gathered downstairs and Zaza saw that the two men she particularly disliked were amongst them.

Then, just as the Professor began to ask what time Emile Pouget was expected, he arrived.

Zaza thought he looked like a clerk. At the same time, there was something about him which gave him a character and a personality which were different from those of the other men sitting round the table.

Almost at once, as soon as he had reached the Professor's side, he sat down beside him and started to tell him of the success of *Le Père Peinard* and the way he was inciting his readers to harass the Bourgeoisie.

"I am telling them to commit theft and arson," he boasted, "to counterfeit bank-notes, to destroy the houses of the rich, and, if they are conscripts in the Army, to desert."

The Professor looked astonished, but Zaza had the idea that he did not believe what he was being told and thought, as she wished to think, that Emile Pouget was just showing off.

"They hate me! They are afraid of me!" Emile Pouget cried. "But all Paris reads me, and the circulation of *Le Père Peinard* increases week after week."

The men sitting at the table listened raptly to what Emile Pouget was saying, but before the Professor could reply, Pierre Beauvais said quietly:

"I think the discussion which is going to break out at any moment should wait until after we have finished our dinner. The Professor has promised his niece, *Mademoiselle* Zaza, that tonight we shall hear some of the poems which several gentlemen round this table have written, and we also want to hear the Professor play. After all, we must not forget that Symbolism embraces music as well as the written word."

There was a murmur of approval although Zaza saw Emile Pouget throw himself back in his seat a little petulantly.

At the same time, as he had barely started his supper, she thought it unlikely that he would leave.

She was right in this, and she smiled at Pierre as one man after another rose to recite a poem. Then the Professor picked up his violin, which Zaza realised Pierre must have brought downstairs for him.

For a moment he cradled it in his arms as if it were a child he loved, then he put it under his chin and played one of the melodies that she had listened to for over ten years.

She knew it was one which always moved the Professor profoundly because it was so beautiful and was a cry from his very soul.

Because he had once been a great master and could still play very much better than most of the young professionals, there was silence in the Café des Champs.

It was the silence that is the greatest tribute an artist can draw from his audience.

And when the Professor stopped playing there was that silent moment when those who had been listening to him came back from the dream-world into which his music had transported them to the mundane and commonplace.

They applauded, wine was passed round the table, and they raised their glasses to the Professor.

"You are one of the greatest!" a man said.

The Professor's old face flushed with pleasure, but Zaza saw Emile Pouget turn down the corners of his mouth, looking mocking and cynical.

He did not speak, however, and as if by his silence he drew attention to himself, someone said:

"What about you, Emile? What will you give us?"

Because there was an aura of success about him, everybody listened for his reply.

"I will sing you a song," he said, "a song which you all know, one we will never forget."

He paused for a moment, then said:

"I presume you all remember Ravachol?"

"Yes, yes!" they all cried.

"Before he was executed two years ago," Emile Pouget went on, "he bequeathed his name to the most famous of all our songs because it is based on the *Carmagnole,* the *Ça Ira* of our greatest revolution."

He said no more but rose to his feet, and as he did so, he put his hand on the Professor's shoulder, who knew what was expected.

Emile Pouget began to sing and the Professor accompanied him.

> **Dansons la Ravachole*
> *Vive le son, vive le son!*
> *Dansons la Ravachole*
> *De l'explosion.*

---

*Let us dance the Ravachole,
Long live its music!
Let us dance the Ravachole
Of the explosion.

It was a song Zaza had never heard before, but she had heard about it and knew that because it was so revolutionary her father had banned it from being sold or sung in Melhausen.

When Emile Pouget sat down, the applause from the whole Café was as great as the applause had been for the Professor.

Then, as is usual after a moment of emotion, everyone began to talk at once.

At the Professor's table it was obvious that Emile intended to hold the floor and let no-one else say very much. As his voice rang out, Pierre rose from his seat and came down to stand behind Zaza's chair.

He bent down and whispered very softly in her ear:

"I think this is where you and I escape. Wait for a few minutes before you follow me. Then come to the Entrance-Hall."

He moved away the moment he had spoken, and Zaza thought excitedly that he intended to take her somewhere where they could dance.

She had not forgotten that that was what he had promised, and when she had been changing before dinner she had put on the lightest and prettiest of the gowns she had brought with her.

She could not help wishing that she had one of her really elaborate and beautiful ball-gowns with which she could dazzle Pierre, but she knew that they were so elegant, so expensive, that even if she had one of them in her carpet-bag she would not have been brave enough to wear it.

Even her plainest afternoon-gown looked very elegant and perhaps too expensive to be a garment one would expect a poor Professor's niece to wear.

Yet Zaza reasoned to herself that Pierre Beauvais did not know whether the Professor was well off or poor, and it was not a question he would be likely to ask.

"Besides," she told herself, "as far as he is concerned, I might have a father who has made a lot of money by manufacturing something important like trains or—firearms."

As she thought of the latter she shivered.

Ever since she had come to Paris there had been too much talk of people being killed, shot, bombed, assassinated.

It all added up, Zaza thought, to the same thing —murder—and it was a crime which frightened her.

Now she was glad that she could slip away from the dinner-table not only because it was a wonder beyond wonders to be with Pierre, but also because she would not have to listen to Emile Pouget.

She was quite certain that he was not a Symbolist in any shape or form but an avowed anarchist.

He was also, she suspected, an opportunist who was cashing in on the present fashion of anarchism simply because it would pay him to do so.

'The Professor should not be mixed up with such people,' she thought to herself. 'He is far too trusting, far too idealistic, and has not enough common sense to see it through as do men like Emile Pouget.'

Emile Pouget was at the moment pounding the table with his fist, and as everybody was listening to him wide-eyed they took no notice when Zaza pushed back her chair.

She was certain that they were so hypnotised by what they were hearing that they did not see her leave.

She ran up the stairs and found Pierre waiting for her.

He smiled when she appeared and she felt her heart turn over in her breast because he was so attractive and because a magnetism she could not begin to put into words drew her to him.

"Did anybody ask you where you were going?" he enquired.

"Nobody was in the least interested in me," Zaza replied.

"I will tell you how interested I am when we are alone," Pierre said in a low voice.

He put his arm through hers and drew her towards the door.

"What about Uncle François?" she asked. "How will he get to bed? He must not try to walk yet."

"Everything is arranged," Pierre replied. "The Concierge has agreed to warn him in an hour's time that he must not become over-tired, and he will give him another hour, and after that, if necessary, he will shanghai the Professor so that he goes to bed whether he likes it or not."

Zaza laughed.

"I am sure he will protest very volubly, but at the same time he must not become exhausted."

"No, of course not," Pierre agreed.

As they were talking Zaza realised that they were waiting for one of the porters to get them a *voiture*.

When it came Pierre helped her into it, then sat down beside her on the back seat.

The *voiture* started off and he took Zaza's hand in his, turned it over, and kissed the palm.

His lips were passionate and possessive and she felt herself quiver with the excitement she had felt this afternoon when he had kissed her lips.

"I love you!" Pierre said. "Every moment I am away from you, every second you are not with me, passes with the slowness of a century, and when I see you again you are even more beautiful than you were before."

"Time passes . . . slowly for me too," Zaza said in a small voice, "but . . . Pierre . . . I am frightened about my uncle being . . . mixed up with men like *Monsieur* Pouget."

"I agree, he is a very unpleasant specimen," Pierre replied. "I was very surprised when I learnt he was joining the Professor and his friends this evening."

"He invited himself," Zaza said quickly.

"Are you sure of that?" Pierre enquired.

"Quite sure," she said. "I was there when that man Laurent, whom I do not like, came upstairs to tell the Professor that Emile Pouget wanted to meet him."

She paused for a moment before she went on:

"He made it sound very flattering, so my uncle was delighted, but I did not expect him to be so horrible."

Pierre did not reply and she realised that he was thinking.

"Pouget has done a great deal of harm," he said after a moment, "and the Government is worried by the violent tone of the anarchists' propaganda produced by people like him, who keep exhorting the working people to rise against their masters and destroy the social system."

"Surely that . . . could not . . . happen?" Zaza asked in a frightened voice.

"There has already been one violent revolution in France," Pierre replied.

"That was over a hundred years ago, as Emile Pouget reminded us tonight."

"The message is still the same. Assassinate! Kill! Destroy the existing order, with nothing sensible to put in its place."

Zaza's fingers tightened on Pierre's.

"It frightens me!"

"I will look after you."

He spoke impulsively, then he added in a different tone: "If it is possible for me to do so."

"Why do you say it like . . . that?" Zaza enquired.

Pierre did not reply. Then as she waited he said:

"It was just a manner of speaking."

But she knew that was not the truth.

Their carriage came to a standstill and Pierre said:

"We have arrived!"

They stepped out of the *voiture,* Pierre paid the driver, and walked into a *Café chantant* which was called the Jardin de Paris.

When Zaza went inside she knew, as she had anticipated, that Pierre had brought her to a place that was very different from the *Caf conc's* of which

she had read and was in fact patronised by a far
smarter clientele than she had seen at the Café
des Champs.

They were given a table outside the Café on
a terrace in the centre of which was a dance-floor
overlooked only by trees and decorated with flowers
growing in the garden.

It was lit by Chinese lanterns and was extremely
attractive.

Pierre ordered some wine, then rose and held
out his hand.

"Come and dance," he said, "and, as I promised,
later this evening I will teach you the Polka."

It was fun, Zaza thought, being taught anything
by Pierre, but she preferred to dance the waltz with
him when they could swing round and round with
his hand on her waist.

She knew that as partners they suited each other
perfectly and the rhythm of the music was the
rhythm of their heart-beat.

They danced and talked, and danced again, and
Zaza started when Pierre said:

"It is getting late. I think I should take you
home."

She gave a little sigh.

"It has been so wonderful being here. Must we
leave each other?"

"That is for you to decide," he replied.

"I want to stay but perhaps you will feel tired
tomorrow."

"That was not exactly what I meant," he said.
"Never mind, we will leave and we will talk about
it somewhere quiet."

Zaza looked at him in perplexity. She was not
certain what he wished to talk about.

He paid the bill, then outside the Jardin de
Paris they found a *voiture* and she heard Pierre give
the driver some instructions.

She did not ask what they were and when Pierre
stepped into the carriage he put his arm round her
and drew her close against him.

"Thank you," Zaza said. "Thank you so much

for taking me to such an attractive place. I love dancing with you, and I realise it was very respectable."

"What were you expecting?" Pierre asked. "A place like the Moulin Rouge?"

Actually that was the sort of place that Zaza knew was patronised in Paris by men who visited the Gay City, even her father.

She had overheard him, when he thought she was not listening, telling a friend who was staying in the Palace what he had thought of the high-kicking at the Moulin Rouge and the women who danced the "Can-Can."

She had heard him speak of somebody called *La Goulue*, whose dancing was the height of depravity, and he had related how she had been described as a "Messalina, a monstrous beast, a Vampire—a creature of incarnate degradation."

Zaza knew that Pierre would not have taken her to a place where women like that performed. At the same time, she could not help feeling that he was restricting her, preventing her from being free as the Countess Glucksburg might have done.

"What are you thinking about?" he asked.

Zaza answered him truthfully.

"I was thinking that I want to be free. Not the sort of freedom that Emile Pouget is seeking, but the freedom of the true Symbolists, who would encourage me to be myself."

"What do you want as yourself?" Pierre asked in his deep voice.

He put his arm round her as he spoke and felt the little quiver that went through her.

"As myself," Zaza answered, "I want to fly into the sky and dive down into the sea. I want to feel ...unrestricted and as...happy as I...felt today when you ... kissed me."

She only whispered the words, but he heard them.

"That is what I want too, my darling, but you are sure, absolutely sure, that that is what you want?"

He asked the question with an almost solemn note in his voice and Zaza said:

"Of course I want it! That is why I came to Paris. That is why I was thinking this evening how very . . . very lucky I was to have met . . . you."

She thought he would kiss her, but instead he paused for a moment as if he was trying to make up his mind.

Then he stood up in the carriage which was half-open and attracted the attention of the driver.

"The Hôtel des Champs," he said.

Zaza wondered what instructions he had given previously, but she did not want to ask questions when Pierre's arms were round her.

Only when they actually reached the Hotel did she feel sad that the evening was over.

'I must not be greedy,' she thought to herself. 'There are other nights, and I shall see him tomorrow.'

There was only a sleepy night-porter in the vestibule to hand over their keys, yawning as he did so, and Zaza and Pierre walked up the stairs side by side.

As they reached the third floor Zaza asked:

"Do you think Uncle François is in bed asleep?"

"I am sure he must be by this time," Pierre answered, "but to set your mind at rest I will just peep in to make sure."

They stopped at the Professor's door and Pierre turned the handle very softly.

The room was in darkness but there was no mistaking the sound of heavy breathing that came from the bed.

Pierre shut the door again and smiled at Zaza.

She could not see him clearly in the light of the one gas-lamp which was all that was left burning on the landing at night.

"Your uncle has been put to bed, just as I ordered," he said.

He took Zaza's key from her as he spoke and unlocked her door, then he lit not the gas-lamp but a candle beside the bed.

"That will not be very much light," Zaza said.

"It is enough for what we want," he replied.

He shut the door behind him, took off his coat, and threw it on the ground. Then held out his arms and Zaza moved towards him, lifting her face to his.

"Good-night, darling Pierre. It has been a wonderful . . . wonderful . . . day. I have never been so . . . happy."

"Do you love me?" he asked.

"You know I do. I love you more than I can ever . . . say."

"I want you to be mine!"

"I am yours . . . all yours," Zaza replied passionately. "Every bit of me . . . belongs to . . . you."

"Not completely," he answered.

His arms pulled her closer still, he looked down at her face, and she thought there was a question in his eyes

Then, as if there was no need for words, he was kissing her, kissing her with slow, passionate kisses that seemed to lift her, as he had done this afternoon, into the sky where they were above the world and there was nothing but themselves and their love.

It was so perfect, so rapturous, that Zaza did not realise that still with his mouth holding hers captive Pierre was moving her towards the bed.

Only when he tumbled her backwards onto it did she give a little cry.

For a moment she was too surprised to protest. He lifted her feet onto the counterpane, then threw himself down beside her.

His lips found hers and as he kissed her demandingly, fiercely, insistently, she felt his hand through the thin silk of her dress, moving against her breasts.

It was then that she began to struggle.

"No, Pierre . . . no!" she cried, without even thinking what she should say.

He was kissing her neck and he raised his head to ask:

"What are you saying?"

"You . . . must . . . go," Zaza said breathlessly. "It is not . . . right . . . that you should be in . . . my bedroom."

Pierre raised himself on his elbow. He was looking down at her and Zaza could see the expression in his eyes.

Somehow she was suddenly conscious that she was lying full length on the bed and he was lying beside her.

She felt it was wrong—very wrong—and the rapture she had felt when he kissed her vanished.

Instead she felt guilty and, in some way she did not understand, apprehensive.

As if he knew she was afraid Pierre said:

"My darling, I would not frighten you, but you know I want to make you mine, and you told me you wished to be free."

"Do you . . . mean . . ." Zaza began incredulously.

Then quickly she added:

"No . . . I did not mean . . . that we should do anything . . . wrong or wicked."

"Do you really think it would be wrong or wicked when I love you and you love me?" Pierre asked. "As far as I am concerned nothing could be more right."

"M-making . . . love would be . . . wrong if we were not . . . m-married."

She knew as she spoke that Pierre stiffened and there was a sudden silence—a silence in which she thought she could hear her heart beating.

"I told you," Pierre replied, "that I could offer you nothing but my love, and you said that was all you wanted."

"It is . . . and it is marvellous . . . perfect . . . an ecstasy I cannot explain, that you should . . . love me," Zaza said, "but I know we should not be . . . lying together on this . . . bed. That is . . . wrong!"

"Why should you think that?" Pierre asked, and she thought there was something hard in his voice.

It was difficult to talk to him when she was lying on her back and he was looking down at her,

but she said in a hesitating voice because she was
trying to find words to explain:

"I do not know ... because no-one has ever told
me ... what happens when ... two people make love
... and if it was with you ... it would be ... very
wonderful ... but I know that the Church and therefore God would think ... we should be ... m-married
first."

"And if we cannot be married, then you are
saying that you no longer love me?"

"No, no! That is not true!" Zaza cried. "I love
you ... I love you with all of me! I did not know
that love could be so marvellous ... and when you
kissed me I felt it was ... sacred."

Her voice died away because she felt it was
impossible to explain what she was feeling or indeed
what she wanted.

Her whole body throbbed and yearned for
Pierre, and because he was so near he sent through
her strange sensations which she did not even know
existed.

And yet somewhere at the back of her mind
was the conviction that their love must be perfect
and they must not spoil it by doing anything that
was wrong.

But why should it be wrong?

It was all such a muddle, impossible to sort out
at this moment with Pierre so near to her that she
wanted his arms round her and his lips on hers.

At the same time, she had the feeling that a
great gulf had suddenly opened between them when
she had least expected it, and if she fell into it she
would be lost forever.

Then to her consternation Pierre slowly got off
the bed and walked to the window.

He pulled back the curtains and above his head
Zaza could see the glitter of the stars.

He stood looking out, and after a moment she
sat up, knowing that she was trembling and feeling
that she had lost something infinitely precious.

"Pierre!"

Her voice broke on the word.

He did not reply and after a moment she said:

"I ... I am ... sorry I ... upset you ... but I did not ... mean to."

He did not answer and Zaza could bear it no longer.

She jumped off the bed and ran towards him.

"Pierre! Pierre! she cried incoherently. "Do not stop loving me! I do not think I could ... bear it if you did."

There was a frantic note in her voice and as she looked up at him beseechingly he saw the fear and the bewilderment in her face.

Gently he put his arms round her.

"It is all right, my darling," he said, "I still love you. In fact it would be impossible to stop loving you."

"Do you mean that ... do you really ... mean that? You are not ... angry with me?"

"I am not angry," he said. "I only find it a little hard to understand why you are here with your uncle, who does not know how to look after you, and talking about freedom in a manner which is very misleading."

"How ... could it be ... that? How could I have ... misled you?"

Pierre looked down at her searchingly. Then as he saw that she really did not understand, he pulled her close against him and with his cheek against her hair he looked out into the darkness.

"Oh ... Pierre ... what have I said ... what have I ... done?"

It was the cry of a child and he knew that she was not very far from tears.

"Go to bed, my precious," he said after a moment. "We will talk about it tomorrow, but not to-night."

"I shall not be ... able to sleep ... if I think you no longer ... love me."

Zaza's face was turned up to his again and he heard the little tremor in her words as she spoke and could see that there was a suspicion of tears in her eyes.

"I love you! Of course I love you!" he said. "Far too much for my peace of mind, and far more than I ever intended to love anybody!"

It was as if the words burst from him. Then he said in a very different tone:

"Good-night, Zaza. Go to sleep. Forget everything, except that we have had a very happy evening together and we love each other."

"You are quite . . . sure you are not . . . angry?"

"Quite, quite sure."

"Perhaps I was . . . stupid . . . perhaps I should have . . . let you do what you . . . wanted to . . . do."

She felt him draw in his breath. Then he said:

"No, you were right, quite right! So do not torture yourself."

She waited for him to say more, but when he did not do so, she said:

"Please . . . will you kiss me . . . good-night . . . as you kissed me . . . before?"

She lifted her lips to his and again he looked down at her face for a long moment. Then he drew her close and kissed her.

For a moment she thought the magic had gone and he no longer wanted her, then as her mouth trembled against his, his lips became passionate and possessive as they had been before.

As she clung to him he kissed her fiercely, demandingly, almost as if he were fighting her with kisses.

She felt that she surrendered her whole body, mind, and soul to him, but he released her, picked up his coat, walked towards the door, and pulled it open and left her without saying another word.

She heard his footsteps going down the passage. Then because he had gone she felt the tears gather in her eyes even while at the same time her whole body was pulsating with the wonder and joy he had awakened in her.

She felt almost as if there were flames within her, setting her on fire.

Yet some part of her brain cried out because she had lost what she wanted, even though she was not quite sure what it was.

"I love you! I love you!" she whispered aloud.

She could not decide even to herself whether her voice was a cry of ecstasy or of despair.

Chapter Six

Zaza awoke and felt there was something wrong. Then she remembered what had happened last night and a sudden depression swept over her like a dark cloud.

She had gone to sleep in tears, knowing that she had upset Pierre and feeling that she had been wrong even though he had said she was right.

It was all so muddled in her mind: her love for him and the fact that her instinct had told her that although their love was perfect and sacred, what he had been about to do would spoil it.

He had said that she had been misleading and she supposed that he had misunderstood what she had said about seeking freedom.

Now she asked herself how, as the Princess Marie-Celeste, she could have permitted a man she barely knew to kiss her and feel as if he carried her into the heart of the sun.

Yet she had known in her innermost heart that she was behaving outrageously.

What would her mother have thought of her? And she had no need to ask herself what her father and the Countess Glucksburg would have made of her behaviour.

"I love him! I love him!" she whispered.

Because she could not wait another moment to see Pierre, she sprang out of bed and started to dress.

It was a little later than usual because she had

118

not fallen asleep until dawn had broken over the roofs of Paris.

"I will wait for him and have breakfast with him as usual," she told herself consolingly.

At the same time, she hurried into her gown, barely stopping to look at her reflection in the mirror, and opened the door of her bedroom.

As she stepped into the passage she heard voices in the Professor's room and thought with inexpressible relief that Pierre was with him.

For a moment she paused, patting her hair into place, then took a deep breath to try to control the frenzied beating of her heart.

As she lifted her hand to knock on the Professor's door, it opened and she saw that Dr. Sachet was just leaving.

"*Bonjour, Mademoiselle!*"

He looked at her with undisguised admiration and it was with difficulty that she found a voice in which to reply because she was so disappointed that he was not Pierre.

"*Bonjour, Monsieur.*"

She managed to smile, although it was with an effort.

"I have good news for you," the Doctor said. "Your uncle's ankle has recovered, and he can now do anything he wishes as long as he does not walk too far or too fast. As I told you, we have very good *fiacres* in Paris which will carry him wherever he wishes to go."

The Doctor paused for her to reply and Zaza said:

"I will see that he does not over-exert himself, *Monsieur.*"

"I am sure you will look after him admirably," the Doctor said, "and I have with me what I promised you."

He took a large packet from his pocket and held it out to her.

"The powdered bones!" Zaza exclaimed.

"There is enough there for two months," the Doctor said, "and I have written my friend's address on a piece of paper. If you write to him for more, he will send it to you in Melhausen."

"Thank you, thank you very much!" Zaza said. "I am sure it will help my sister."

"I am quite certain it will," Dr. Sachet agreed, "and you must let me know how she progresses."

"I will do that," Zaza replied, wondering if it would be possible.

"Now I must hurry to my other patients," he said. "*Au revoir,* Professor. If I cannot come to see you tomorrow, it will be the next day, but do not forget that you have promised to play for me before you leave Paris."

"I will keep my promise," the Professor replied, "and thank you. You are a good friend."

The two men smiled at each other, then the Doctor left the bedroom.

The Professor sat up in bed.

"I am going to get up, *ma Princesse,*" he said. "Then we will see some of Paris together. I have so much to show you, so much that I want to see myself."

"That will be . . . lovely," Zaza replied.

She hoped that her voice did not sound as dismayed as she felt.

If she was with the Professor, how could she be with Pierre? Every nerve in her body was calling out for him, longing for him.

"Go and have your breakfast," the Professor said, "and I will join you as soon as I am dressed."

Zaza was only too anxious to follow his suggestion as she was sure that Pierre was waiting for her in the Restaurant.

She put the packet of bone-powder in her bedroom, then ran down the stairs as quickly as she could.

She almost burst into the small Restaurant to find it empty except for the elderly waiter who had her table ready for her in the corner where she had sat before.

"*Bonjour, M'mselle,*" he said. "You are late this morning."

"A little late," Zaza agreed. "Where is *Monsieur* Beauvais?"

"*Monsieur* has left, *M'mselle*. He had breakfast very early this morning."

For a moment Zaza was still with shock.

"L-left?" she questioned in a voice that did not sound like her own.

"He had an appointment, *M'mselle*, and he was in a great hurry."

The waiter pulled out a chair for Zaza and with an effort she made herself sit down.

For one terrifying moment when he said that Pierre had left she had thought he meant that he had gone for good.

If he had an appointment, that was a different thing altogether.

She felt sick with the shock of what she had thought, and when the waiter brought her coffee and a hot Brioche she sipped the coffee quickly, feeling it somehow helped her.

Other guests from the Hotel came into the Restaurant and the waiter went to attend to them and Zaza was grateful that she did not have to go on talking.

All she could think of was that she would not see Pierre this morning and the Professor intended to show her Paris.

She wondered what he would say if she told him that she had no wish to see Paris, no wish to go anywhere, no desire to discuss Symbolism, music, or anything else except with Pierre.

"I must behave properly," she told herself sternly.

At the same time, she wondered how it could be possible.

*   *   *

Driving in an open *fiac*re along the quay beside the Seine, Zaza did not see the sun shining on the water or feel the breeze rustling the leaves of the trees which lined the road.

All she could see was Pierre's face and all she could hear was his voice.

'I am hopelessly,... crazily,... wildly in... love,' she thought.

Then almost like a blow came the question:

"What are you going to do about it?"

"What can I do?" she asked herself.

Sooner or later she would have to return to Melhausen.

She could not remain in Paris forever and she had the feeling that when her father began seriously to worry about her disappearance he might connect it with the absence of the Professor.

Even if she hid in Paris under an assumed name, the Professor was known to too many people and the Melhausen Police would have no difficulty in discovering where he was staying and with whom he was associating.

When her mother was alive they had often talked at meal-times of the Professor's qualifications and the fact that besides being a musician he was also a poet.

Looking back, Zaza could remember her father saying irritably:

"Symbolism! What does that mean, I would like to know! It is nothing but a fancy name for some long-haired romantic who thinks he can string words together and make them jingle."

The Grand-Duchess had laughed.

"We have to move with the times, Frederik," she had said. "Symbolism is very up-to-date and becoming fashionable even among our friends."

"Music I can tolerate," the Grand-Duke had replied, "but I draw the line at poetry. If you intend to introduce it into the Palace, then I warn you, I shall have a pressing engagement elsewhere."

Her mother had laughed at him, but Zaza was certain that her father, who had a retentive memory, would not forget that besides being a music-teacher the Professor was a Symbolist.

If they wished to find him they would come to Paris, and there it would be impossible to disguise the fact that the Professor was accompanied by a

niece who looked surprisingly like the Princess Marie-
Celeste.

'I shall have to return to Melhausen before the
Professor gets into any trouble,' Zaza thought.

She had the feeling that although he had often
railed against living in Melhausen, finding it not as
progressive as he thought Paris to be, he would
not now, as he had in the past, be as keen to live
with the friends who had written to him all these
years.

It was not what he said but what he did not
say that told her he was in fact sadly disillusioned.

If things had been as he expected, she was
quite certain that as they drove along the sunlit
streets he would be telling her what had been discussed last night and would be inspired into a fiery
diatribe.

Instead he was surprisingly quiet about his
friends, talking only of Paris itself, its history and
its beauty.

They looked at the outside of the Cathedral of
Nôtre Dame. Then the Professor walked slowly and
carefully inside to sit in a back pew and point out
to Zaza some of the more ancient pieces of carving,
telling her to absorb the mystery of what he said was
one of the most esoteric buildings in all France.

Then they drove to look at the Arc de Triumph
and from there down the Champs Élysées to where
under the chestnut-trees children play and there was
a man selling a great variety of coloured balloons.

Its very gaiety made Zaza long even more for
Pierre.

She wanted him with her, she wanted to feel
him close beside her, his eyes looking into hers, his
deep voice paying her compliments which made her
heart turn over in her breast.

"I know a little Café where we can eat," the
Professor was saying.

Zaza gave an exclamation.

She had been hoping that Pierre would be with
them for luncheon.

"That would be very pleasant, Professor," she said aloud, "but could we first go back to the Hotel? Perhaps it would not be far out of our way."

"Yes, of course," the Professor agreed.

Zaza told the driver to take them to the Hôtel des Champs and when they reached it she said to the Professor:

"Why do you not wait in the carriage? I will not be long. I am only going to run up to my bedroom."

"I am in no hurry," the Professor said. "In France one can eat at any time."

He spoke with satisfaction and Zaza remembered the strictly punctual meals at the Palace when her father was furious if anyone was even a half-a-minute late.

She jumped out of the *fiacre* and ran into the Hotel.

The Concierge was reading a newspaper behind his desk.

"Has *Monsieur* Beauvais returned yet?" Zaza asked anxiously.

"*Non, M'mselle*, or if he has I have not seen him."

Zaza felt her spirits droop.

"Please make sure," she pleaded.

The Concierge called the porter, but the man was positive that *Monsieur* Beauvais had not returned since he had left early that morning.

Zaza went up to her bedroom feeling despondent and not far from tears.

Could it be her fault that Pierre had gone without leaving her a message? Surely he would understand how worried she would be?

As she reached her bedroom she stood staring at her reflection in the mirror, seeing the anxiety in her blue-grey eyes and in the droop of her lips.

Yesterday she had been so happy. Today she felt as if the sunshine had gone and she was in a fog of indecision.

There was no Pierre to reassure her and she

could only go downstairs again to where the Professor was waiting.

Afterwards she could never remember what they had seen or what they had done in the afternoon after they had lunched in a small Restaurant.

There the *Patron* had greeted the Professor with loud cries of joy and provided them with a very special meal and a bottle of wine with his compliments.

Because she loved the Professor, Zaza made every effort not to let him know what she was feeling.

She knew how much coming to Paris meant to him, and she did not want to spoil it for him by a lack of enthusiasm and interest in what he had to tell her.

She forced herself to act as if she were listening to every word he said, and although her eyes were on his face and she looked the attentive pupil she had always been, her whole being was crying out for Pierre and every hour that passed made her more apprehensive in case she had lost him.

'Why was I so stupid . . . so foolish?' she asked in her heart.

When they returned to the Hotel he was still not back and she felt afraid with a sudden terror that she might never see him again.

As the Professor moved slowly up the stairs, holding on to the bannister and resting his injured ankle every third step or so, she suddenly turned and ran down to the little Hall.

"Are you quite certain," she said to the Concierge in a voice that trembled, "that *Monsieur* Beauvais has not left for good? He has not taken his luggage with him?"

"Oh, no, *M'mselle*," the Concierge replied. "*Monsieur* Beauvais's luggage is still in his room and his bill is unpaid."

He gave her an understanding smile and said in a father-like manner:

"Now don't you worry yourself, *M'mselle*, *Monsieur* will be back for dinner and in time to join your uncle and his friends in the Café this evening."

"Please tell him when he arrives," Zaza said, "that I wish to speak to him."

"I will tell him, *M'mselle*. Don't you worry yourself."

As she ran up the stairs again Zaza thought how reprehensible it was that she should have revealed to the Concierge her feelings for Pierre.

But she did not care what he thought. All she wanted was to be sure that Pierre would return and she would see him again.

There was no sign of him before dinner, and when she and the Professor went down to the Café there was only the usual collection of his friends, including Laurent and Boisseau, whom she disliked.

Tonight she was thankful that Emile Pouget was not there.

Even so, the conversation almost immediately turned to what Laurent and Boisseau called "desirable action," and a voluble and noisy argument ensued between them and the Professor, supported by his more moderate friends.

Almost before it started Zaza had ceased to listen.

Her eyes were drawn irresistibly to the doorway which led into the Hotel and every newcomer who came through it made her heart leap as for one fleeting second she thought it might be Pierre.

The evening dragged on and on, and she had no idea if she ate anything or whether the dishes she ordered went away untouched.

All she could think of was that she had lost Pierre and she felt as if an icy hand was squeezing her heart until she could no longer feel anything but an ever-deepening pain.

"Pierre! Pierre! Why do you not come?"

Tonight it was the Professor who at midnight declared he was tired after his first day of activity and thought he should retire to bed.

Because there was still a hope that Pierre might arrive even at such a late hour, Zaza wanted to stay in the Café, but she knew it would have been impossible for her to do so without the Professor.

Reluctantly she followed him as he hobbled up the stairs, obviously tired almost to the point of exhaustion.

When they reached his room she lit the gaslight for him.

"Shall I help you, Professor?" she asked. "Or can you manage by yourself?"

"Of course I can manage, *ma Princesse*," he replied. "I am well again now. Only a trifle fatigued. Tomorrow I shall be my old self and we will visit the Academy together. That is definitely something I wish to show you."

"That will be delightful," Zaza said. "Goodnight, Professor. Sleep well."

"God bless you, my child," he replied.

Zaza left him and went to her own room.

She could not believe that the whole day had passed and there had been no sign of Pierre.

Why had he gone? Why had he left her? How was it possible that he could be so cruel, knowing that because she loved him she would worry over his disappearance?

It suddenly struck her that perhaps he had had an accident.

Suppose he, of all people, had been blown up by one of the anarchists' bombs?

She felt desperate at the very idea. Then she told herself that if there had been an explosion in the City that day, Laurent and Boisseau would have spoken of it at supper.

She could not remember one word they had said, but she was sure that if there had been talk of an outrage, an explosion of any sort, it would have attracted her attention.

She walked up and down her room for a long time without undressing, then she sat on the bed, feeling as if she sent out a cry from her very heart to Pierre and somehow wherever he was he must hear it.

Could his love have vanished so completely

overnight? Could they be no longer attuned to each other, no longer part of each other as they had seemed yesterday?

She could not believe that such a thing had happened. It was impossible.

"I love you! I love you!" she called. "Hear me! Come to me! I want you!"

She felt as if she threw out invisible waves from her very soul and they winged towards Pierre and found him and he heard her message.

"I want you! I want you!"

The words, although she had not spoken them aloud, seemed to echo and re-echo round the small room, then came back to her and she thought despairingly that she could not reach him.

It was several hours later when finally she undressed and got into bed.

The night was almost over, the stars were fading in the sky, and already there was a faint glow in the East.

She was so tired and so miserable that almost as soon as her head touched the pillow she fell asleep.

* * *

Zaza was aware of a sudden inexplicable happiness seeping into her like a shaft of sunlight.

She could feel Pierre's lips on hers and she thought as it brought her to consciousness that she was dreaming, and yet it was a dream that she could not lose.

Then she realised it was reality.

Pierre was there and he was kissing her!

She made a little murmur of happiness and he raised his head.

"Wake up, darling!"

She opened her eyes and saw him beside her, his head silhouetted against the pale morning sunshine coming through the window.

"Pierre! You are back!"

It was a cry of happiness.

"I am back," he said, "but, darling, you have to

get up. You have to leave Paris at once—you and the Professor!"

The way he spoke swept away the last vestige of sleep and Zaza opened her eyes wide.

"What did you . . . say?" she asked.

"You have to leave Paris immediately!"

"But . . . why? What are you . . . telling me? What has . . . happened?"

"The President has been assassinated!"

For a moment what Pierre had said did not penetrate Zaza's mind. Then she heard her own voice say incredulously:

"It . . . cannot be . . . true!"

"It is true," Pierre declared. "He was assassinated in Lyons and the Government will arrest all those who are known to be anarchists or connected with them."

Zaza gave a little cry and sat up in bed.

"You mean . . . the Professor?"

"The Professor and his friends are all too well known not to be taken into custody. That is why, my darling, you must get out of Paris and out of France."

She sat looking at him wide-eyed, and as his eyes rested on her he said in a very different voice:

"You are very lovely first thing in the morning, just as I thought you would be. I did not realise your hair was so long."

For the first time Zaza was conscious that she was wearing only a thin, almost transparent nightgown and her hair was falling over her shoulders.

Instinctively she put her hands to her breasts as if to protect herself and Pierre smiled.

"I would like to stay here and tell you how beautiful you are and how much I love you," he said, "but it is more important that I should save you both. Hurry, my precious! I will go and wake the Professor."

He turned towards the door but Zaza gave a little cry.

"If we are to go back to Melhausen," she said, "when will I ever see you again?"

"I have been worrying about that myself," Pierre

answered, "but somehow we will find a way, and it will certainly be easier than visiting you in prison, so hurry!"

He went from the room as he spoke, shutting the door behind him, and Zaza stared after him for a moment as if it was impossible to think of anything but him and that they would be separated.

Then she knew that what he had told her meant that it was imperative that she should not only get the Professor to safety but also herself.

What would happen if she was taken prisoner and it was discovered who she was?

She could imagine the scandal it would cause not only in Melhausen but amongst the other Royal Houses of Europe, most of which were related in some way or another to her father and mother.

The idea of a Royal Princess going off on her own to Paris accompanied only by a man would be a scandal as explosive as any anarchist's bomb, and Zaza was well aware that because of it she would be ostracised for the rest of her life.

For the first time since she had run away from the Palace she was aware of the full implications of her revolutionary action and the consequences that might arise from it.

Because she was so frightened she dressed at an unprecedented speed, then bundled everything she possessed into the carpet-bag.

She hardly glanced at herself in the mirror as she arranged her hair and put on her straw hat.

As if Pierre had timed exactly how long she would take, she was just placing her brush and comb on top of her other things when there was a knock on the door and he came in.

"The Professor is ready," he said, "and has gone downstairs to pay the bill."

He came to her side as he spoke and took the carpet-bag from her hands and strapped it together.

Then he looked at her.

Her eyes met his and, without thinking, driven only by the intensity of her feelings, she flung herself against him.

"Oh, Pierre! Pierre!" she cried. "How can I leave you? And surely if we run away you . . . must do the same . . . thing? They might . . . arrest you!"

"They will not do that," he replied.

There was something in the way he spoke which made her draw herself a little way from him, although her arms were still round his neck.

"How can you know that for certain?" she asked, then guessed the answer.

"You are . . . connected with the . . . Police?"

She could barely say the words and they were little more than a whisper.

She knew as she spoke that it was the truth, and yet she thought Pierre would deny it, until he replied:

"Something like that. That is why I know it is important for you to leave."

"You were . . . spying on the Symbolists! Oh, Pierre, how could you?"

"Not on the Symbolists," he said, "but on men like Emile Pouget. The real Symbolists like your uncle would never do anyone any harm."

"Why . . . why?"

"It is a long story," he answered. "You have to trust me."

"I did trust you," Zaza said, "but now I . . . think you are an . . . enemy."

Pierre smiled.

"You know that is untrue where we are concerned. Whatever I am, whatever you are, we still belong to each other and I love you. I love you, my darling, as I have never loved anyone before and will never love anyone again!"

He put his arms round her and pulled her against him as he spoke, and as his lips came down on hers, she thought wildly that nothing mattered.

He could be Policeman, Judge, Executioner—it was immaterial. He was Pierre and she loved him.

Because he was kissing her, everything in the world vanished except him and the sensations he aroused in her.

She could feel her body pulsating against him

and her lips surrendered themselves completely to
his.

Then without speaking, just releasing her and
picking up her bag, Pierre took her hand and drew
her towards the door.

As they went down the stairs Zaza's heart was
beating against her breast and she knew that if he
asked her to stay with him she would do so, whatever
the consequences now or in the future.

When they reached the Hall there was no sign
of the Professor. Then she saw that the night-porter
had already found him a *fiacre* and he was standing
beside it, waiting for them.

Pierre drew her across the pavement towards
the Professor and lifted her bag into the carriage.

"There is a train to Melhausen at five-thirty," he
said.

"Good! And thank you!" the Professor replied.

He stepped into the closed carriage and Zaza
turned to Pierre.

"You are . . . not coming with us?"

He shook his head.

"Please . . ."

"I cannot," he replied.

"Then when shall I see you again?"

The words seemed to burst from her lips.

"I will come to Melhausen, I promise you," he
said. "I cannot tell you exactly when or how, but I
will come."

He saw the agony in her eyes and she thought
there was an inexpressible pain in his.

For a long moment they spoke to each other
without words as if they both knew that words were
unnecessary.

Then Zaza felt Pierre's lips on her hand, and
almost before she could realise what was happening,
he had helped her into the carriage and it drove off.

She bent forward, expecting that he would stand
on the pavement to see them go, but he had already
turned and all she could see was a fleeting glimpse
of him walking through the door of the Hotel.

She wanted to call after him—she wanted more than anything else to run back and ask him to kiss her just once more.

Then she knew that this, as if like the death-knell, was the end.

She would never see him again. Even if he came to Dorné, they would not be allowed to meet.

Far away, as if it came from another world, she could hear the Professor's voice.

"How could I have guessed—how could I have known that this would happen?" he asked. "That they should kill the President is insane!"

He paused for a moment before he went on:

"*Monsieur* Sadi Carnot was a good man. To kill him will achieve nothing, except as Beauvais has said, all those connected with the anarchist movement will be arrested."

The Professor groaned.

"To think I have involved you in such a situation! You of all people! You who trusted me!"

There was so much pain in the old man's voice that Zaza knew she had to comfort him.

"It is all right, Professor," she said. "Pierre has saved us. When we return to Dorné no-one will know where we have been or connect us in any way with what has happened in Paris."

"We must make sure of that," the Professor said. "But how could I imagine that I would lead you into such danger? You who should have nothing to do with such *canaille* from the gutters—for they are nothing else!"

"It was not your fault," Zaza said. "You went to Paris to talk of poetry and freedom of the mind. How could you or I imagine that we should find ourselves involved with people who would want to kill and destroy their fellow-beings?"

"It is monstrous!" the Professor murmured.

He was obviously so deeply upset that Zaza tried to console him in every way she could.

"Once we are across the border into Melhausen," she said, "no-one will connect us with what happened in Lyons, and although Pierre did not say so, the President's assassination may not be announced in the newspapers until later in the day."

"Then how did Beauvais learn of it?" the Professor enquired.

Zaza had no intention of telling him that Pierre was connected with the Police, but she found herself thinking about it and finding it incredible.

Yet she supposed she might have been suspicious from the very first moment she saw him.

He had been walking with the officials investigating the injuries of the passengers on the other train.

He had said he was a Symbolist, but while he talked as if it meant a great deal to him, he had somehow not looked the part and was certainly very unlike the Professor's so-called Symbolist friends.

Some of them were undoubtedly poets and what they had recited in the Café had a beauty that matched what she had expected and what she had found in the poems of Mallarmé and Verlaine.

But everything they said had been the very opposite of the ideals they should have upheld and the dream-like mystery that was so much a part of their creed.

Zaza remembered the Professor telling her years ago that Symbolism, with its emphasis on the mysterious, unseen, spiritual world of the soul, was the aim not only of the poets but of certain artists and musicians like himself.

How could that possibly be allied to the violence, the cruelty, and the terror employed by the anarchists?

She could understand how shocked and disillusioned the Professor was by what had occurred, and she knew it would have been far better for him to have remained in Melhausen with his dreams instead of being shattered by reality.

She knew a very great part of his feeling of upset was due to the fact that she had become involved, and when the train drew out from the station she said:

"Whatever has happened, Professor, I want to thank you for taking me to Paris, because it has been for me the most wonderful and the most exciting adventure."

"Do you really mean that, *ma Pincesse?*" he asked.

"I mean it with all my heart," Zaza replied, "and I shall never forget what it meant to me personally. It will be something to remember for the rest of my life."

There was a throb in her voice that was unmistakable, and the Professor looked at her sharply and for the first time forgot his own troubles.

"You are not saying," he asked after a moment, "that young Beauvais meant something—special to you?"

They were alone in the carriage and Zaza was able to answer him.

"I love Pierre," she replied. "I love him with all my heart! I thought when I left the Palace that I would never know love and it would never mean anything in my life."

The Professor gave an exclamation of dismay.

"But, Your Royal Highness! This should never have happened!"

"It *has* happened, Professor, and there is nothing you, I, or anyone else can do about it!"

"But it is impossible—you and young Beauvais—who is nothing but a poet!"

Zaza did not reveal that he was other things as well, but merely said:

"What he means to me is something I shall always remember and treasure in my heart ... until I die."

As she spoke she could not help the tears coming into her eyes, and as if he could find no words in which to express his own feelings, the Professor reached out and took her hand in his.

"My child," he said, forgetting protocol, "I blame myself for this. It should never have happened. I am a stupid, foolish old man to do anything so outrageous as taking you to Paris."

"I have told you, Professor, it was the most wonderful thing that ever happened to me in my life."

"But it should not have happened!" the Professor protested, "You are Royal; yet, because you are so intelligent, so understanding, I was thinking only of your soul and I forgot how beautiful you are."

He made a little gesture with his hands that was typically French.

"What man worthy of the name would not fall in love with you? And yet I never anticipated that such a thing could happen."

"It happened . . . it just happened," Zaza said, "and it was so wonderful . . . so perfect that I . . . never want to forget."

She spoke in a dreamy voice and lay back agaist her seat, thinking of Pierre.

When they had arrived at the station the Professor had taken First Class tickets, and as there was only one coach with two First Class compartments on the train, it looked as if they would be alone for the whole journey.

The train was certainly not one to be patronised by rich or important travellers.

It was very slow, stopping at every station, and carried for the most part farm-folk conveying their warés to market, or Commercial Travellers with cases of samples which they piled on the racks of the Second and Third Class carriages.

After they had been travelling for a little time Zaza saw that the Professor had fallen asleep, and she thought that the shock of being awakened by Pierre with the news of the assassination of the French President had exhausted him.

Despite the fact that she had slept so little during the night, she was not tired.

She could only feel despairingly that the train was carrying her away from everything that mattered to her in life, and yet she was sensible enough to know that there was nothing she could do about it.

She must go back to the Palace and pick up her life where she had left it, somehow appeasing her father's anger at having run away, and prepare herself for marriage to a man whom she had never seen and for whom she could never feel anything, whatever he was like, because he was not Pierre.

She knew that having loved so overwhelmingly, so whole-heartedly, a man who she believed was the other part of herself, it would be impossible for her ever to love in the same way again.

Her love for Pierre was perfect, part of the divine, and could come only once in a lifetime.

She wondered if Pierre felt the same. Perhaps men were different—she did not know. She only knew that now they were divided by a gulf that nothing could bridge.

He had said he would come to Melhausen and she supposed that as he knew the Professor came from Dorné, it would be easy to find him.

Then the Professor would tell him the truth and he would have to leave without seeing her.

She would remain a memory in his heart, but time would make him forget because he would have his career and perhaps a number of other interests, while she would have only her "painted prison" for the rest of her life.

The train trundled on through France and there were passengers who got on and off at the various stations, but no-one came near their carriage.

The Professor awoke, talked for a little while in a shocked voice about what had occurred, then slept again.

Zaza sat looking with unseeing eyes at the passing landscape, seeing only Pierre, hearing his voice, feeling the touch of his lips.

"I love him!" she said over and over again to the rumble of the wheels.

They reached the border and she roused the Professor to remind him that they required their passports.

She wondered if by any chance her father had already begun his search for the Professor, but she thought it unlikely.

It was too soon for him to be really worried. He

would still be raging about the Palace at the idea of her going away without his permission.

It was likely to be a week before he really troubled himself as to her whereabouts.

She had already thought about whom she could say she had been staying with, and had concocted a story, although she was sure he would not listen to it, having so much rage to expend before she could open her mouth.

There was no handsome young officer this morning to look at the passports. Instead there was an elderly man who was obviously tired and bored with the whole procedure.

He did not speak but merely inspected their papers and moved on to the next carriage.

"Well, we are home!" the Professor said. "But it is not the way I expected to return! I am despondent about what has happened in my beloved Paris."

"I am still glad we went," Zaza replied.

He looked at her and she thought he was about to speak again of Pierre. Instead he merely sighed, and after a moment she said:

"Once again we forgot to bring any food with us, and I admit, Professor, to feeling hungry, and I would greatly enjoy a cup of coffee."

"Forgive me, *ma Princesse*," he begged. "I am not looking after you as I should. In fact that is something about which I have been very remiss since the moment we left Dorné."

"Nonsense!" Zaza replied. "We will get something to eat and drink at the next station. If I remember rightly, the train stops there for quite a considerable time."

"That is true," the Professor said, "and I will try to find you one of those ham-rolls you enjoyed so much."

They smiled at each other in an almost conspiratorial manner and Zaza said:

"It will be at least three-quarters-of-an-hour before we get there. Go back to sleep, Professor. I know you are tired."

"That is true," he agreed. "I suppose all this excitement has been too much for me at my age."

Almost as if she commanded him to do so, he made himself comfortable in the corner of the seat and linked his hands across his chest.

Zaza pretended to look out the window, because she did not want to talk. She just wanted to go on thinking of Pierre . . . Pierre . . . Pierre . . .

*   *   *

When nearly an hour later the train rumbled into the next station, Zaza looked at the Professor and realised he was still fast asleep.

'I will not wake him,' she thought. 'I will go myself and get something to eat.'

She picked up her bag and realised as she did so that she had stuffed her money into it when she was packing and remembered she had never had time to talk to the Professor about what she owed him for her expenses on the whole trip.

'It is something I must do before we reach Dorné,' she decided.

She walked across the platform a little nervously.

Fortunately, in the buffet there were very few people and she was able to ask for two cups of coffee and two ham-rolls without any difficulty.

She had already selected the smallest of her gold coins with which to pay for them. Even so, there was quite a commotion about finding change.

"Have you nothing smaller, *M'mselle?*" the man behind the bar enquired almost indignantly, as if she were deliberately trying to defraud him.

"I am afraid not," Zaza replied.

Finally he slapped the change down in front of her as if she had committed a crime, and she hurried back to the railway-carriage to find the Professor still asleep.

She either had to wake him or leave him without his coffee, and finally she decided the best thing to do would be to buy him another cup at the next station.

She therefore drank both cups of coffee, put a ham-roll beside him on the seat, and took the tray and cups back to the buffet.

The money she had deposited on them was returned to her and she went back to the carriage feeling that all on her own she had achieved something.

'First the Professor looked after me, then Pierre,' she thought. 'I have really done practically nothing for myself since I left the Palace.'

When the train started off again, Zaza, having finished her ham-roll, looked enviously at the one she had left for the Professor.

It seemed a very long time since she had eaten anything, and last night she had been so perturbed about Pierre that she must have eaten very little. She could not remember.

Then she told herself not to be greedy.

'What I will do,' she thought, 'is to wake the Professor before the next station, and then he can buy himself another cup of coffee.'

She waited until she thought they had been travelling for over twenty minutes before she put out her hand and touched the Professor's.

"Professor!" she called.

He did not move and she pressed his hand with her fingers.

"Professor, wake up!"

He still did not move and she felt a sudden fear strike through her.

"Professor! Professor!"

Now her voice was frantic and she moved to sit on the seat next to him and began searching desperately in his pocket for the little bottle of drops she had given him on the outward journey.

Even as she found it and drew it out she knew it would be useless.

The Professor was dead!

Chapter Seven

Zaza walked languidly along the corridor with the Countess Glucksburg beside her.

"I cannot think, Your Royal Highness, why you spend so much time at the piano when you have no music-teacher," she was saying.

This was a sentence Zaza had heard repeated over and over again for the last four days and she had ceased to listen. She had actually managed to detach herself from hearing a great deal of what went on at the Palace.

She had found, as she expected, that her father roared at her in his rage, not waiting to listen to anything she had to say, as he violently rebuked her for daring to leave the Palace without his permission.

Her detachment had been contributed to by the fact that she was suffering from shock when she arrived at the Palace from the railway station after the Professor's death.

She had known it would not be long before his body was discovered by officials or by other passengers entering the carriage, and she had taken every precaution, not only for her own sake but for his, that she should not be connected with him and that there would be no scandal attached to his death.

When she realised that he was dead and there was nothing she could do for him, she knew she must think for herself.

It was extraordinary, she thought later, how calm she had been and how clearly her brain had worked, even while she wanted to weep bitterly because she had lost the one friend she had in the Palace, the person who had understood her interests and her desire for freedom.

The Professor had been respected in Dorné and his reputation was something which she knew must not be sullied by gossip or scandal.

If there was even a suspicion that he had been accompanied by a young woman on his visit to Paris, it would do him harm even if the truth did not emerge as to who his companion was.

Zaza made her plans, then sat beside the Professor with her hand on his.

"Thank you," she said beneath her breath, "for all the kindness you have shown me ... for the way you have ... helped and guided me these years we have ... worked together. I will never ... forget you ... I shall always be grateful that you took me with you to Paris."

She felt that wherever he now might be, he would understand what she was trying to say and would not reproach himself.

She was very pale, but quite composed when twenty minutes later they came into a small station where there were only two porters.

When Zaza looked out the window she saw that they were both busy at the Guard's Van at the other end of the train. She climbed out of her compartment, holding her carpet-bag, and without anyone being aware of it she moved into the next compartment.

This too, being First Class, was empty, and she travelled alone until the train reached Dorné.

There she descended quickly onto the platform and walked away with the other passengers leaving the train without anyone taking any notice of her.

She hired a hackney-carriage and asked the driver to take her to the Palace.

"Go to the side-door," she added, and knew he

thought she was one of the senior servants, perhaps even a new Governess for the young Princesses.

He set her down at a door which she and Rachel used when they were leaving the Palace for a drive with the Countess Glucksburg or merely going for a walk in the grounds.

Only as she entered the Hall where there were two footmen in attendance was she recognised.

"Your Royal Highness!" one of them exclaimed.

She told the man to collect her carpet-bag from the carriage and walked away down the corridor and up a back staircase to her bedroom.

She hoped she would be able to see her sister before she encountered the Countess Glucksburg, and as she entered Rachel's bedroom she sat up in bed with excitement.

"Zaza, you are back!" she exclaimed. "I was not expecting you so soon!"

"I had to come," Zaza replied, "and I will tell you why in a moment. Tell me first, before we are disturbed, what has happened here."

Rachel laughed.

"You have never heard such a fuss! Papa was in a towering rage when he learnt from the Countess that you had left the Palace. I think she was sorry she had told him, because he was furious with her for not supervising you better."

"He received my note?" Zaza asked.

"Yes, but only after the Countess said she could not find you and had been told by one of the housemaids that your room was unoccupied."

Zaza laughed.

"It sounds the usual twisted channel of communications. What happened then?"

"Papa was very angry. He came and asked me what you were doing. I said I did not know, so he merely contented himself by telling me what he would say to you when you returned."

Zaza made a face.

"I am quite prepared for that."

"Why did you not stay longer?" Rachel asked. "Did you not enjoy Paris?"

"It was wonderful!" Zaza said. "The most wonderful place in the world!"

"I received your letter this morning," Rachel said, "but you did not tell me what you were doing."

"As it only came this morning," Zaza said, "you will not have had time to order the things I have instructed you to have, so I will do it for you. I have also brought with me something to help your back."

"I am sure it will help me," Rachel said, "but I feel better already because you are here. I have missed you, Zaza. I have missed you terribly!"

Zaza put her arms round her sister and kissed her. Then she started to tell her everything that had happened since she had left the Palace, while Rachel listened enthralled.

Only when she had finished did Rachel ask:

"But if the Professor is dead, how will Pierre be able to get in touch with you when he comes to Dorné?"

"Even if the Professor were alive he would not to see me," Zaza replied.

Rachel looked at her almost indignantly.

"Zaza! How can you be so faint-hearted and defeatist? Of course you must see him! You can meet in the grounds at night, or you could go shopping in the town and lose the Countess somehow. It should not be difficult."

"And if I do see him, how will it help?" Zaza asked. "You know as well as I do that if he is connected with the Police he will know how wide the gulf is between us."

"I thought you loved him."

"I do!" Zaza answered. "I love him with all my heart! I love him until I can think of nothing else! But I know he could never marry me even if I asked him to."

"How do you know that?" Rachel enquired.

"Because he would lose his job, whatever it is, and I expect that if he tried to marry me in Melhausen, Papa would have him put in prison and he might even be persecuted in France."

"There are other countries."

"How can we live without money, hunted like thieves? And if we were caught, you know that Papa would drag me back here and shut me up in a Convent or something."

Zaza's voice was bitter. Then she rose from the bed to walk across to the window.

"It is no use, Rachel. I have thought about this very seriously. I have lived for a short time in a magical dream-world, and that is all it can ever be for the rest of my life."

Rachel held out her hands.

"Oh, Zaza, I cannot bear the story not to have a happy ending! I want you to marry Pierre. I want your love to be greater than anything else."

"It is no use," Zaza said, and her voice was infinitely sad. "I am back in my 'painted prison,' and make no mistake, Rachel, it is a prison from which I can never escape again."

She told herself the same thing over and over again, night after night.

She would cry in the darkness, yearning for Pierre to the point where she felt that Rachel was right and she should risk everything to be with him again.

She told herself stories in which she went back to Paris to look for him and when they found each other they ran away to England or Spain—any place where they could escape.

But she knew such ideas existed only in her imagination and could not be translated into reality.

Even if Pierre married her knowing who she was, it would be impossible for them to live without money, nor could they be married when she was under-age and had to have permission from her parent.

"If only we could have been together longer," Zaza would cry. "If only I had more to remember ... more happiness to hide in my heart."

She found herself wishing over and over again that she had not struggled against Pierre when he had lain beside her on her bed.

Then she told herself that if she had belonged to him as he had wanted, perhaps for him it would have spoilt the memory of their love.

She knew so little about men's feelings. She knew only that her lips ached for Pierre and there was a pain in her breast which seemed to intensify every time she thought of him.

Now as they reached the Music-Room the Countess said:

"If Your Royal Highness really intends to practise for the next half-an-hour, I have a great many things that need doing. Will you give me your word of honour that you will not leave this room until I return for you?"

"I promise, Countess," Zaza said meekly.

"You have given me your word, Princess! I will therefore trust you," the Countess said stiffly, "and I will return in half-an-hour."

She went from the room, closing the door so firmly pehind her that Zaza knew she would have liked to turn the key in the lock.

She opened the piano, thinking, as she did so, how much she missed the Professor and how she had loved listening to him talk about Symbolism and freedom of the mind.

Now there was no-one to understand her, she thought mournfully, and she tried not to hear a voice inside her mind which said:

"Pierre is alive! Pierre understands! Pierre can give you everything the Professor did, and so much more!"

She started to play but even the music could not move her as it used to do.

Now the ecstasy she had felt then could only be created when she thought of Pierre. Her fingers seemed lifeless and she knew as she played automatically that the spirit and enchantment which music had brought her in the past had vanished.

When the Countess came back, Zaza stood up and closed the piano-lid.

"You certainly will not be able to play tomorrow or for the next few days, Princess," the Countess said with a note of relief in her voice.

"Why not?" Zaza enquired.

"Have you forgotten that Prince Aristide is arriving on his State Visit?"

As it happened, Zaza had hardly given a thought to the imminent arrival of the Prince.

She had known that he was coming sometime, but she was so intent on her thoughts, her own unhappiness, that the days since she had returned slipped by and she had omitted even to think of the Prince and the reason why he was coming to Melhausen.

Now as she went up to her sister's room and the Countess left them alone, she said to Rachel:

"Did you realise that Prince Aristide is arriving tomorrow?"

"Yes, I did," Rachel said, "but I did not want to remind you of it. I thought it might make you more unhappy than you are already."

"I do not think anything could do that," Zaza said. "Oh, Rachel, do you think Pierre is somewhere in Dorné and has learnt that the Professor is dead and is trying to find me?"

"Why do you not drive to the Professor's house? Perhaps one of his relations is there and could tell you if anyone has called," Rachel said practically.

"You do not suppose the Countess will allow me to do that?" Zaza asked. "Papa would not even let me attend his Funeral, so I am sure I would not be allowed to visit his home."

The Grand-Duke had been quite firm in refusing Zaza's request to pay her last respects to the Professor by being at his Funeral.

"A Funeral is not the place for women," he said, "and after all he was only your teacher."

"He was much more than that," Zaza replied, but her father would not listen.

"You can send a wreath with a message of sympathy."

He spoke sharply as he had spoken to his daughter ever since her return.

But he had accepted her explanation, when finally he had agreed to listen to it, that she had gone to stay with the relations of one of their Governesses because she wanted to think about her marriage to Prince Aristide.

"What is there to think about?" her father had enquired. "You are very fortunate to have a suitor who comes from such a pleasant country. I only wish Melhausen were in the South so that we would not be subjected to the cold we had this winter."

"I was not thinking about the country so much as the man who rules it," Zaza had replied.

Once again her father had not listened, and she knew that even if he did so, it would not help.

She did not now feel frightened or nervous of meeting Prince Aristide. She only felt completely detached from reality as she had been since she returned home.

What did it matter what he was like? What did it matter what happened to her in the future?

She supposed she would go on living, but somehow she would never again feel alive.

"Cheer up, Zaza!" Rachel said. "The wedding will be exciting if nothing else, and perhaps the Prince's Palace will be better than this one. At least you will not have Papa shouting at you!"

Zaza did not reply and after a moment Rachel said:

"Do you know, I think I shall be able to come to your wedding. I am sure I shall be well enough to be a bridesmaid."

What she said held Zaza's attention.

"Do you mean that?" she asked. "Do you feel better already?"

"I realised this morning when I woke that I wanted to get up. In fact I did get up, and I walked round the room. I thought of getting dressed and going down into the garden, but I knew what a row there would be."

"You really feel better?" Zaza insisted.

"I do—I honestly and truly do!"

"You look better," Zaza said. "You have more colour in your cheeks."

Rachel gave a little cry.

"I believe your medicine from Paris is beginning to work!"

"I am sure the diet helps too," Zaza added.

The Chef had been very surprised when she told him what Rachel was to eat, but she made him understand how important the soup was and also the liver.

She had flattered the Chef into believing that only he could make the liver palatable day after day with his inventive imagination.

Now, looking at her sister, she was certain that there was indeed an improvement.

Rachel's skin did not look so transparent and Zaza knew if only by the way she moved her hands and the way she talked that she had more energy.

"How does your back feel?" she asked.

"It does not ache as much as it did," Rachel answered. "Oh, Zaza, if I really get well, I shall thank God every day that you were brave enough to go to Paris."

"I am sure you will get well," Zaza said, "and as soon as you have used up all the bone-powder I shall write to Dr. Sachet's friend for some more."

"And I can be your bridesmaid?"

"I shall refuse to go ahead with the wedding until you are well enough to follow me up the aisle."

As she spoke Zaza thought that perhaps that would give her some respite from being pressed into marriage wth Prince Aristide too quickly.

Yet it was doubtful if she would have any say in the choice of a day any more than she had had in choosing her own husband.

Because she knew how much it would mean to Rachel she said aloud:

"It will be wonderful to have you as a bridesmaid, so concentrate on getting well. We will choose the prettiest gown that has ever been designed so that everyone will look at you and not at the bride."

"That is exactly what I would like," Rachel said, "but it is unlikely, because, darling Zaza, you are much prettier than I could ever be."

Zaza bent to kiss her sister and she thought as she did so that there was only one man for whom she wanted to look pretty, only one man whom she wanted to admire her, and because he would never see her again she was no longer interested in her appearance.

She allowed the Countess to choose the dress she should wear the next day when she was to meet the Prince.

The Grand-Duke intended to meet him at the station, and when it was suggested that he should be accompanied by his daughter, he had said that women were a nuisance on such occasions and the Prince could meet her in the Palace after the State Drive was over.

As usual, the officials bowed to the Grand-Duke's decree.

Zaza, when she heard it discussed, knew that they were thinking that the sooner the future bride and bridegroom were seen in public together, the more excitement it would cause amongst the population.

There was nothing the crowds enjoyed more than a Royal Wedding.

She was, however, well aware that while it was considered an excellent thing that the two Royal Houses should be united, it was at the moment more important to create a contented atmosphere in Melhausen, considering the difficulties that were taking place just over the border in France.

Zaza had read the newspapers avidly since she had returned home.

What Pierre had told her had happened, had been headlined even in the newspapers devoted entirely to Melhausen affairs.

The sensational assassination of the French President had shocked all France, and the Government and the Police in Paris had immediately decided to put all known anarchist theorisers on trial and prove they were directly responsible for all the outrages.

Zaza read that the houses of suspects were searched and a great number of arrests were made, among them being Emile Pouget, who was to be brought to trial within the next two months.

She was surprised, however, to read that despite what was described as the extremely violent tone of the anarchists' broad-sheets and reviews which had caused the class war in Parisian society, only eleven major bomb-explosions had occurred in Paris in the last two years.

But even so, a number of innocent people had died, and she could not really blame the French for taking a strong line against the nerve-war which the anarchists had been waging against the Bourgeoisie.

Her father of course had a great deal to say on the subject.

"The sooner all these damned traitors are guillotined, the better!" he said. "The French Government has been too weak with them up until now, and I assure you, at the first bomb that explodes in Melhausen, I will guillotine every man, woman, and child who has any connection whatsoever with it."

Zaza knew, because he was shouting even louder than usual, that he was afraid.

It made her think that perhaps to fight violence with violence was not really the way to keep the peace, but there was no point in saying so to her father.

She was sure his Ministers were right in thinking that a Royal Wedding in Melhausen would take the minds of the population off anarchy and other revolutionary subjects.

That Dorné would be *en fete* for a wedding would be far more interesting, especially from the women's point of view, and the only person who would really dislike it from start to finish would be herself.

However, there was nothing she could do but accept the inevitable, and she therefore dressed in one of her most elaborate gowns, and with the Countess Glucksburg in attendance she waited with numerous officials of State for the Royal Procession to arrive at the Palace.

No-one seemed to notice, she thought, that she was quieter than usual and that she was very pale and there were dark lines under her eyes.

She supposed that to most of the women chattering round her, she was just a symbol of Royalty and not a person at all.

As long as she behaved in the way that was expected, they would ask no more of her than if she were an automatic machine that played a tune when one turned the right knob.

Last night she had cried for Pierre until she was exhausted. Then, as if for one moment the lethargy that had encompassed her since her return lifted, she found herself feeling acutely miserable in a manner that set every nerve in her body crying out for him.

"Pierre! Pierre!" she had sobbed in the darkness.

She felt as if she went down into a hell all her own in which there was no light and no hope.

Today she had a headache, the lassitude had returned, and she felt that she did not care what happened or what Prince Aristide said or did.

If he refused to meet her when he arrived, she felt she would be the only person who would not be shocked or even surprised.

Perhaps the anarchists were right and the Monarchy was an anachronism which belonged in the past, and in the future there would be no Monarchy, no Bourgeoisie, only the workers who would demand more and give less.

She felt that if only she could discuss with the Professor what was going to happen and what had happened, it would be better. But now she was alone, completely alone, and there was no-one with whom she could talk, no-one to understand, no-one who could explain to her what she wanted to know.

She realised that the Countess had spoken to her and she had not heard what she said.

"I . . . I am sorry," she apologised. "What did you say?"

"I said," the Countess Glucksburg replied sharply, "that their Royal Highnesses have arrived."

Zaza looked round and realised that the Statesmen and their wives had arranged themselves in a long line on either side of the red carpet which led from the door up to the dais to which her father and Prince Aristide would walk.

She stood on the dais with the Countess behind her, waiting to receive them. It was there that she would meet the Prince for the first time.

There was a little murmur at the end of the room which, with its huge crystal chandeliers and spacious proportions, was the biggest Reception-Room in the Palace.

"Here they come!" the Countess hissed with a note of excitement in her voice.

Quite suddenly Zaza felt that she must run away.

She did not wish to meet the Prince, the man she was to marry, the man who doubtless had as little wish to be wed to her as she to him.

The anarchists were right, she thought. All the Monarchies should be swept away; then she could be an ordinary person who could marry someone she loved and have no duties to perform except those of running a home and bringing up children.

'If I had a bomb in my hand at this moment,' Zaza thought, 'I would throw it!'

But she knew that she would neither run away nor behave like a revolutionary.

The training she had undergone all her life would make her behave as she was expected to do, whatever her personal feelings in the matter might be.

For a moment she shut her eyes and thought of

Pierre with his arms round her and his lips on hers, carrying her up into the sky.

Then she could hear the chink of her father's gold spurs as he walked over the red carpet and she supposed the same sound was echoed by the Prince's, and there was the rustle of silk gowns as the ladies curtseyed.

Now they were here, stepping onto the dais.

"May I present my daughter, Marie-Celeste," she heard her father say.

Zaza sank down into a very low curtsey, her eyes on the ground.

She had no wish to look on any man's face except that of the man she loved.

"It is a great honour to meet Your Royal Highness," a deep voice said.

Then as his hand touched Zaza's, she could feel through the kid gloves they both wore the strength of his fingers, and as she rose gracefully from her curtsey she was frozen into immobility.

They were Pierre's eyes she saw, Pierre's face, Pierre's hand that was touching hers!

If she was astonished so was he!

They both looked at each other incredulously, feeling as if the whole world had tumbled about their ears, and yet at the same time they could see and hear nothing but themselves.

From somewhere very far away Zaza heard her father saying:

"You must welcome His Royal Highness to Melhausen, Marie-Celeste."

She knew as he spoke that he was puzzled that she was not uttering the appropriate words of welcome as he had instructed her to do earlier in the day.

But Zaza could think of nothing except that Pierre was there, and she realised as he gazed at her that he was as tongue-tied as she was.

They each knew one thing and one thing only: they had found each other again.

*   *   *

Zaza crept slowly and carefully along the corridors in which some lights had been lowered and many extinguished.

She had slipped down to a side-entrance so as to avoid the main Hall where the night-porters would be on duty.

Now she entered one of the Reception-Rooms on the ground floor and crossing it, opened one of the long French windows which led into a small private garden at the side of the Palace.

This garden was enclosed by a wall and was therefore excluded from the usual march of the sentries round the Palace.

She moved towards the fountain in the middle of it, and as she did so, someone came from the shadows on the other side.

"Pierre!"

She could barely breathe his name before he was beside her.

"It is not . . . true!" she said. "It cannot be . . . true that it is . . . really you!"

"Do you suppose I am not saying the same thing?" he asked in his deep voice. "How can Marie-Celeste be my own beloved, beautiful Zaza whom I have been frantically trying to find ever since she left Paris?"

"Is that . . . true?" Zaza enquired.

"I will tell you all about it in a moment," he said, "but first I want to make sure you are real and I am not dreaming that Marie-Celeste is the freedom-loving girl I kissed beside the Seine."

As he spoke his arms went round her, bringing her closer to him.

"Shall I make sure?" he asked.

Then his lips were on hers.

As he kissed her, Zaza felt a new ecstasy and the wonder she had felt before from his kisses. But now they were more intense, more vivid, because she had been so sure that she had lost him forever and would never again know the happiness he aroused in her.

He kissed her until once again everything was forgotten except themselves, and he carried her high in the sky and she felt as if they were one with the stars.

It was a long time later when he drew her to a marble seat half-hidden amongst the exotic flowers which filled the small garden.

As they sat down he did not take his arms from her.

"I thought I would never... see you again," Zaza said and her voice trembled as if she was still afraid.

"I thought I would never find you," the Prince replied. "I have had one of my trusted servants searching Dorné for the past week, but the only niece he could discover who bore the Professor's name was over thirty and, he assured me, very plain and homely in appearance."

Zaza gave a little laugh.

"I borrowed Gabrielle Dumont's passport."

"That is what I suspected must have happened when I was not fearing that you had never existed at all and had only been part of my imagination."

"I thought the same," she said. "Oh, Pierre, I thought I would never see you again. How can this have happened?"

"That is what I am asking myself," he said.

"When you had... found me... what were you ... going to do... about me?"

"That was something I was going to discuss with you."

He spoke seriously, and as she looked up at him in a puzzled way he said:

"I intended to ask you, my darling, if you would marry me morganatically."

"And what about... Marie-Celeste?"

"I would have said firmly that my affections lay elsewhere. It would have annoyed your father and the Councillors both in Valoire and in Melhausen, but that did not trouble me."

"And you... thought I would... agree?"

"I was very, very afraid you would refuse."

"Oh, darling Pierre ... do you suppose I would have ... refused you ... anything? How ... could I?"

"You refused me once," he said quietly.

She hid her face against his shoulder.

"I am not going to tell you ... how often I have ... bitterly ... regretted being so ... foolish'"

"It was not foolish," he said. "It was absolutely right. I know you felt, as I did afterwards, that it would have spoilt something perfect and wonderful in every way. You were right when you said it was wrong."

She turned her face up to his and he looked down at her.

Her eyes were very large and dark in the moonlight, but her lips were inviting his and there was a faint smile on his face as he said:

"Now everything is right, my precious, and exactly as it should be."

"I am ... afraid," Zaza said.

"Afraid?" he questioned.

"That it is too perfect ... too wonderful. Perhaps at any moment we shall be ... blown up by an ... anarchist's bomb because ... fairy-stories do not happen in real life."

"This fairy-story does," Pierre said firmly, "and I have a feeling now, after what had happened in France, that any explosion that will happen to us, my precious little love, will be only the explosion of love."

"That ... is what has ... happened."

"Exactly!" Pierre agreed. "And I will protect you, look after you, and love you for the rest of our lives."

Zaza pressed herself a little closer to him.

"How soon can we be ... married?" she asked. "I wanted to put off my wedding to wait. But now I ... want to be your ... wife."

"I had no intention of marrying the Princess Marie-Celeste in Melhausen," he said, "but now I can think of nothing more wonderful than that she should be my wife, and as quickly as it is possible for a marriage to be arranged."

"Perhaps we can point out that the quicker the wedding takes place, the less likely there is to be any outbreak of anarchy in Melhausen," Zaza suggested. "It is an argument to which Papa would listen."

Then before the Prince could reply she said:

"You have not told me what you were doing in Paris or how you are connected with the Police."

"There is so much we have to learn about each other," Pierre said. "All I can think of at the moment is that I have you in my arms and I no longer have to go on fighting my own Prime Minister and Council. When I told him I wanted a morganatic marriage, he was so angry I thought the whole Government would resign!"

"You have still not answered my question," Zaza said.

"That is simple," Pierre answered. "I offered to help the French, who were in a frantic state of nerves about their anarchists, simply because I am a Symbolist."

"What has that to do with it?"

"I knew the anarchists were using the Symbolists as a cover in their encroachment on the intellectuals of the City, and because I have a reputation in the South as a poet, the President, whose death I deeply regret, asked me to discover which of the clubs were really dangerous to the Constitution."

Pierre sighed before he went on:

"He was a very fair-minded man and he had no wish to persecute those who were really doing no harm but were advocating a freedom of speech in which he believed."

Zaza moved a little nearer to Pierre.

"It was very brave of you. I am sure if men like Pouget, Laurent, and Boisseau had been . . . aware who you . . . were, they would have somehow . . . disposed of you."

"It was a risk I took because it rather interested me to do something different," Pierre explained.

"So you too wanted to be free!"

"It is something I have always believed in," he said. "But let me say, my precious, that it is not the sort of freedom I think advisable for very beautiful young women."

"If you are going to shut me up in a 'painted prison,'" Zaza said, "I shall...refuse to...marry you."

His arms tightened round her.

"Do you really believe I could lose you?" he asked. "I assure you, now that I have found you again, you will never escape!"

He was holding her so close that Zaza could feel his heart beating against hers, and she wanted to say that she was completely and absolutely his prisoner for life.

But because she felt she must show a little spirit she murmured:

"I must have...freedom to...think."

"That perhaps I will allow you," Pierre conceded "but you will never again have the freedom to go to Paris either alone or with a doddering old man who cannot look after you properly, and kiss a young man you hardly know beside the Seine."

"That is not fair!" Zaza protested. "You know I would never kiss anyone but you, and how could I ...help letting you kiss me when I already...belonged to you?"

"You still feel that?" he asked in his deep voice.

"You know I do," she answered, "you know I belong to you, that I am a part of you. When I thought I would never see you again I felt as if I had died."

He knew from the pain in her voice how much she had suffered, and he moved his lips against the softness of her cheek as he said:

"You really do love me?"

"I have...loved you for a...million years."

"I thought a love like ours no longer existed in this particular dimension."

"Now that we have...found each other again ...how can we be estranged?"

The Prince did not answer because he was kissing first the corner of her mouth, then her small chin.

"Are you really... shocked," Zaza asked in a whisper, "because I let you ... kiss me?"

"I am not shocked, my lovely one, and I agree with you, it was because we knew we were already a part of each other," Pierre replied. "But I warn you, I shall be a very jealous husband. If you ever look again at anyone as you looked at *Monsieur* Beauvais, I promise I will beat you and shut you up in one of the turrets of my Palace, where no-one shall ever look on you again, except myself!"

Zaza gave a little laugh.

"You do not think I would mind that, as long as we were together? Oh, Pierre, I want to be with you... I want to be... close to you, like this... or even... closer."

Pierre's arms tightened until they hurt.

"If you say things like that," he said, "I shall carry you away with me tonight, regardless of a scandal, and we will be married in Valoire, and there will be no Royal Marriage to make a Roman Circus for the population of Melhausen."

"Papa would be furious!" Zaza exclaimed.

But she was thrilling to his words, quivering at the strength of his arms and the touch of his lips moving against her skin.

"I love you, I love you so wildly," Pierre said, "that it is difficult to think straight, to remember what I have said or not said and what plans I have agreed to. All I can think of is that I have found you when I was doing everything possible to prevent my marriage from taking place to a girl called Marie-Celeste."

Zaza gave a little laugh of sheer happiness.

"How can you now explain to them that you wish to marry her... and very quickly?"

"That is quite simple," Pierre replied. "Any man who has looked at you, my darling, would understand my feelings. But remember—I was not supposed to have seen you until today."

"Nor I you," Zaza said. "How can it be true that you are really Prince Aristide and my Pierre? I just do not believe it."

"I will make you believe it as soon as we are married," Pierre said. "And I find it hard to believe, my lovely one, that suddenly there are no more difficulties, no more heart-searchings, no more sleepless nights."

"Last night I cried for you ... I told you how ... unhappy I was ... why did you not hear me?"

"Perhaps it was because I was so unhappy myself," Pierre replied. "I stayed with some friends just outside the boundaries of Melhausen in France, and the man who I had sent to look for you came to tell me how fruitless his search has been. It was then that I became really frightened and knew that if I had lost you my whole world would come to an end."

"Darling, darling, you have found me!" Zaza cried. "We are together. I can love you and look after you, and you will look after me and I need never be afraid again."

"And the anarchists?" Pierre enquired.

"Their bombs do not frighten me," Zaza said, "at least ... not very much. It was the idea of being regimented, encroached on, virtually imprisoned as I have been here since Mama died, that terrified me. That is why I wanted to be free to think, to breath ... yes, and to be with people who understood poetry."

"And now you are to marry a Symbolist poet," Pierre said. "I shall write volumes of poems to your beauty, and perhaps they will bore you as much as you have been bored already."

"Do you think that possible?" Zaza asked.

"No," he replied. "I think, my darling, we have so much to talk about, so much to discuss, besides so much love to give each other, that if we lived for a thousand years it would not be long enough to say and do all the things we want."

"That is what I think too," Zaza said. "But perhaps, because you have done so much more than I have, you will after a time find me rather ... dull."

"I think that very unlikely," Pierre said, "but if

we should find that happening, we will go away
somewhere alone and just be Symbolists together,
finding the mystery and dreams of our souls and of
course, more important still, our hearts."

"Oh, darling, you make it sound so wonderful!"
Zaza exclaimed. "And what could be more magical
and adventurous than being married to you?"

She put her arm round his neck as she spoke
to draw his head even closer.

Then his lips captured hers and she felt the
passion she had aroused in him almost like a fire
burning inside her.

As he kissed her the fire rose within her to
flicker through her body like little flames that seemed
to rise higher and higher, and she knew not only
spiritually but physically that they were a part of
each other, a man and a woman complete.

"I love you . . . I love . . . you!" she whispered as
Pierre raised his head.

"I adore you!" he said. "Now, my precious, because I intend to look after you and not allow you
ever again to do anything so outrageous as going to
Paris in search of freedom, I am going to send you
to bed."

"Oh, no! I do not want to leave you."

"Very soon you will never leave me," he said.
"We will be together by night and by day, and then,
my dearest little love, I will teach you about the
freedom of love."

"I would . . . like that," Zaza whispered.

"But now, because I will not have you talked
about or have you involved in a scandal of any
sort, I am sending you to bed. It will be an agony
not to meet you here every night of my stay here
in your father's Palace, but it is something we must
not do."

Zaza moved against him.

"Now you are talking to me like the Countess
Glucksburg and Papa," she said. "I went to Paris with
the Professor to escape from being ordered about
and from always having to do the 'right thing' because of my 'position.'"

Pierre suddenly took his arms from her and held them wide.

"You are free!" he said. "Completely free if you wish it! You can refuse to marry me and I will accept that we are not suited to each other. But if you love me, then love will make you understand that freedom does not consist only of rebelling against the order of things. Freedom exists in love because love gives willingly and wholeheartedly."

For a moment Zaza hesitated.

Then she knew that what he was saying was right and was what she had really been trying to find.

She flung herself against him, holding on to him closely.

"All I want is your love," she cried, "and as long as you love me I will do ... anything you want. I will obey you, but please ... never stop loving me ... because that I could not ... bear."

"I shall always love you," Pierre said gently, "and because I love you I have to protect and look after you."

"And because I love you," Zaza said, "I will do ... whatever you tell me to do."

She knew by the smile on his face that she had said what he wanted her to say, and as she looked at him she gave a little cry of sheer happiness.

"I love you ... I love you!" she cried. "Oh, Pierre ... teach me to be sensible and wise ... teach me to be ... everything you want as your wife."

"I will simply teach you to love me," he said, "then everything else will fall into place."

"You are sure?"

"Quite sure!" he answered. "And I shall love you, my darling, until the stars fall out of the sky, the seas run dry, and the world comes to an end!"

He spoke the words almost as if they were a vow.

Then his lips were on hers, holding her captive, and yet she was a very willing prisoner.

As he kissed her with a fiery, demanding passion she felt that she had now found the freedom she had sought, the freedom which took her into the mystical dream-land of the Symbolists, the freedom which existed in the fire of love and in the divine glory of it.

'I am free,' she thought as Pierre's arms tightened about her, 'and I will love ... love ... love ... until there is nothing else except love in the whole universe.'

ABOUT THE AUTHOR

BARBARA CARTLAND, the world's most famous romantic novelist, who is also an historian, playwright, lecturer, political speaker and television personality, has now written over 200 books.

She has also had many historical works published and has written four autobiographies as well as the biographies of her mother and that of her brother Ronald Cartland, who was the first Member of Parliament to be killed in the last war. This book has a preface by Sir Winston Churchill.

Barbara Cartland has sold 100 million books over the world, more than half of these in the U.S.A. She broke the world record in 1975 by writing twenty books, and her own record in 1976 with twenty-one. In addition, her album of love songs has just been published, sung with the Royal Philharmonic Orchestra.

In private life, Barbara Cartland, who is a Dame of the Order of St. John of Jerusalem, has fought for better conditions and salaries for Midwives and Nurses. As President of the Royal College of Midwives (Hertfordshire Branch), she has been invested with the first Badge of Office ever given in Great Britain which was subscribed to by the Midwives themselves. She has also championed the cause for old people and founded the first Romany Gypsy Camp in the world.

Barbara Cartland is deeply interested in Vitamin Therapy and is President of the British National Association for Health.

Barbara Cartland

The world's bestselling author of romantic fiction.
Her stories are always captivating tales of intrigue,
adventure and love.

☐	12841	THE DUKE AND THE PREACHER'S DAUGHTER	$1.50
☐	12569	THE GHOST WHO FELL IN LOVE	$1.50
☐	12572	THE DRUMS OF LOVE	$1.50
☐	12576	ALONE IN PARIS	$1.50
☐	12638	THE PRINCE AND THE PEKINGESE	$1.50
☐	12637	A SERPENT OF SATAN	$1.50
☐	12273	THE TREASURE IS LOVE	$1.50
☐	12785	THE LIGHT OF THE MOON	$1.50
☐	12792	PRISONER OF LOVE	$1.50
☐	12281	FLOWERS FOR THE GOD OF LOVE	$1.50
☐	12654	LOVE IN THE DARK	$1.50
☐	13036	A NIGHTINGALE SANG	$1.50
☐	13035	LOVE CLIMBS IN	$1.50
☐	12962	THE DUCHESS DISAPPEARED	$1.50

Buy them at your local bookstore or use this handy coupon for ordering:

Barbara Cartland

The world's bestselling author of romantic fiction. Her stories are always captivating tales of intrigue, adventure and love.

☐	11410	THE NAKED BATTLE	$1.50
☐	11512	THE HELL-CAT AND THE KING	$1.50
☐	11537	NO ESCAPE FROM LOVE	$1.50
☐	11580	THE CASTLE MADE FOR LOVE	$1.50
☐	11579	THE SIGN OF LOVE	$1.50
☐	11595	THE SAINT AND THE SINNER	$1.50
☐	11649	A FUGITIVE FROM LOVE	$1.50
☐	11797	THE TWISTS AND TURNS OF LOVE	$1.50
☐	11801	THE PROBLEMS OF LOVE	$1.50
☐	11751	LOVE LEAVES AT MIDNIGHT	$1.50
☐	11882	MAGIC OR MIRAGE	$1.50
☐	11959	LORD RAVENSCAR'S REVENGE	$1.50
☐	11488	THE WILD, UNWILLING WIFE	$1.50
☐	11555	LOVE, LORDS, AND LADY-BIRDS	$1.50

Bantam Book Catalog

Here's your up-to-the-minute listing of over 1,400 titles by your favorite authors.

This illustrated, large format catalog gives a description of each title. For your convenience, it is divided into categories in fiction and non-fiction—gothics, science fiction, westerns, mysteries, cookbooks, mysticism and occult, biographies, history, family living, health, psychology, art.

So don't delay—take advantage of this special opportunity to increase your reading pleasure.

Just send us your name and address and 50¢ (to help defray postage and handling costs).

BANTAM BOOKS, INC.
Dept. FC, 414 East Golf Road, Des Plaines, Ill. 60016

Mr./Mrs./Miss_____
(please print)

Address_____

City_____State_____Zip_____

Do you know someone who enjoys books? Just give us their names and addresses and we'll send them a catalog too!

_____

Mr./Mrs./Miss_____

Address_____

City_____State_____Zip_____

_____

Mr./Mrs./Miss_____

Address_____

City_____State_____Zip_____

FC—9/78